What Readers Are Saying About

The Runaway Pastor

Because 'burn-out' is such a problem for those in the helping professions, this novel blurs the line between fiction and non-fiction to identify with all who need to rediscover the "why" of what they do.

—Gloria Gaither
Author, Speaker and Songwriter

We live. We love. We doubt. We believe. We suffer. The ride can be confusing, even frightening. And sometimes, we run.

While it may be true that no two journeys of faith are alike, Pastor David Hayes hits on essential, common conflicts within each of us, between ourselves, our families and God. Pastor Hayes has never been afraid to let his heart speak, whether from the pulpit, at his blog site, or alongside a friend in pain, which I have been. The Runaway Pastor is a fictional vessel for this gifted communicator to surface a message of truth that resides deep within our hearts and resonates with those of us who wish to somehow find and know grace.

—Jeff Stoffer,
Editor
American Legion Magazine

Loved *Runaway*! It read like a Grisham novel. Exciting and fast paced! Couldn't stop reading.

I read it with tears because some days I would like to disappear and have a new identity. It will strike a nerve in most everyone…because perhaps most everyone is caught up in the world of survival.

I started reading this late in the evening. I didn't stop till I finished the 7th chapter at 2:30 AM…….Can't wait to finish!

I can't wait for the rest of the book. I love the characters, their development, their back-stories…very three dimensional.

This book has hope bleeding through each page.

Where is chapter 8, and the rest? I've gotten sucked into this story!

My pastor-dad gave his life to the church. While he was doing this, I was playing baseball, soccer, playing in the band at school, in plays, etc...and he missed most of them. This story is taking me back to priorities.

I just can't tell you how moved I am. I loved it!

Thanks for a vivid, at times raw (emotionally) presentation of the complex issues that can drive a pastor to despair.

(For several months the first seven chapters were posted on www.runawaypastor.com)

THE RUNAWAY PASTOR

The Runaway Pastor
Copyright © 2009
David S. Hayes

www.runawaypastor.com

ISBN: 978-0-975866

Sydney Lane Press
A Division of Mark Gilroy Creative LLC
Mailing Address:
2000 Mallory Lane
Suite 130-229
Franklin, Tennessee 37067

Jacket and Interior Design: Michele Meyer
Cover Photo: Nate Valesquez/www.sxc.hu

The characters in this novel are purely fictional and do not reflect the life and events of specific real life individuals.

Printed in the United States of America

THE
RUNAWAY
PASTOR

A NOVEL ———————

DAVID HAYES

SYDNEY
LANE
PRESS

FRANKLIN TENNESSEE

ACKNOWLEDGEMENTS

When I sat down to write this book, an unmistakable pattern was developing in my conversations with hurting pastors: Several were indicating a deep desire to simply run away. I was recovering from a disabling confrontation with burnout. And I had recently counseled with a successful business owner, a Christian man, who had indeed run across three states before turning his pickup and stuffed wallet back toward home and family. *The Runaway Pastor* was a desperate attempt to empty myself of the question, "What if?"

This novel exposes the unique agonies many clergy experience. It is my hope that it will encourage pastors who are on the sidelines, feeling they have failed. And perhaps it will help some who remain in the fray to be true to their gifts and their families, and thus find they are being true to God.

I want to thank those who have helped me on this journey. Several volunteered to read, edit and encourage me with the manuscript. Special thanks to Mariruth, Rod, Jo Ann, Gloria, Duane, Zena, Chisato, Paul, Alyssa and my wife—Shelly. Dozens of others commented at my blog (www.runawaypastor.com), and encouraged me along the way. I am grateful.

I had never experienced the intense and rewarding efforts involved in a professional edit of a manuscript. I appreciate so much the work of Jessica Inman (of Mark Gilroy Creative, LLC) who patiently and with great insight edited, coached and encouraged as we worked through the month-long process of fine-tuning this book. Mark Gilroy was instrumental in helping me bring the best out of the characters and storyline during the content development phase.

I dedicate this—my first book—
to my dear wife of thirty years, Shelly;
and to all of the people in Brown County, Indiana
who allow me to pastor them.
You live with, and sometimes through,
my passionate desire to see Christ's church be all it can be.
I will always love you dearly.

chapter 1

LOST

Wednesday afternoon: 12:50

The truth was he had sold out. It was the coward's way. But it was, at least, a way out. His head was spinning as he boarded the red line, just down the street from the hospital. He was headed toward the city center. Trent needed to get lost, and he had a plan to disappear. The way he saw it, he was already lost. Long lost.

Six hours earlier

The ringing telephone marked the end to a fitful night. Natalie opened her eyes to see her husband stepping away from the bathroom sink, wiping the phone side of his face clear of shaving cream. Grabbing the telephone from the nightstand, he answered. "Hello." His voice hadn't warmed up for the day, and he had to repeat himself. "Pardon me. Hello." Much clearer.

Natalie's look said, *Who would call at this time on Monday morning?*

Reentering the room, Trent set the telephone on the dresser and grabbed a pair of socks from the drawer. "Gotta run." He was hopping in a circle, trying to reach his foot with the end of the sock. Throwing on a pair of pants, he made a move toward the door, then stepped back to say good-bye.

9:00 AM

"Hello, Pastor Atkins. How are you this morning?" Rhonda Simpson had been the church secretary for twenty-four years now, outlasting four pastors and plenty of crises. She managed to run a tight ship, while remaining the friendly and enthusiastic presence of the front office at Baylor's Bend Community Church.

"Very well, thanks, Miss Simpson." He wasn't very convincing.

Rhonda just shook her head. Pastor Trent was truly an enigma. As he took off his raincoat and stepped past her into his office, she could tell he was under incredible stress. Yet his presence in the room was still gentle and authentic. When he had first arrived in Baylor's Bend, several women had mentioned that he was "easy on the eyes." But soon all such talk was gone. It wasn't that Trent had lost his good looks—his lean, yet sturdy build or his soft gray eyes. It was just that when people got to know Trent, his physical appearance was overshadowed by his deep, loving heart. When they were near him, they knew they were safe, embraced in some invisible cloak of God's love.

"Need some quiet," he now said tiredly. "I had another emergency meeting with Jerry from the bank this morning. Church ledgers are bleeding." Jerry Oswald was a banker who attended Baylor's Bend.

"I'll hold your calls."

"Thank you, Rhonda," Trent said as he shut himself into the office.

Sitting at his desk, he ran his fingers up through his hair, squeezing them together so he could feel the pull on his scalp.

Was he going mad? It was a crazy idea. He took a moment to massage his scalp and neck, but it was no help. It was too early to have such a raging headache.

Checking his desk, he noticed the "while you were out" notes, a stack of twenty-some calls he needed to make. He had sorted them into stacks: congregational leaders, the bishop, creditors and collectors, and mysteries—just good people needing something.

"Not now, please not now," he muttered to the wall. Another stack lay to the right. A conference in California, only $295 per person! (Plus airfare, lodging, food. . . .) Faces smiled up from the brochure. Healthy people telling him to come away with his wife and fall in love all over again. *Right,* he thought. *I'll come and get my marriage fixed up in one weekend, and you'll make your living on my crisis.*

His cell phone rang. He spoke into the mouthpiece for a moment about hope, hanging on, about trusting and praying. He referred to a scripture and said a brief prayer. He made a note and added it to a file. The office phone was ringing in the background.

He sat and wondered for the thousandth time what else he could do—*anything* to get out of the job. He'd had opportunities and offers for consulting jobs; he could be a fund-raiser, a church-growth guru, a worship transition specialist, or whatever. There were a million needs at the top of pastors' minds. But he had no passion left for any of these. Lately Trent had been preoccupied with one thing: escape.

His feelings of bitterness ran deep. The church had become a marketplace. Singers, speakers, and writers offered to come and inspire his congregation. TV preachers were constantly bidding for dollars and fame from the television screen. Others were hawking books, CDs, board games, greeting card lines, videos, dolls, paintings, and the list could go on and on. It seemed that there were big bucks to be made, all in the name of Jesus—meanwhile, his church was behind on its mortgage payment.

How could they get rich in the name of the One who had nothing? The One who said, "Foxes have holes and birds of the air have nests, but I have no place to lay my head"? He wondered if that was his true feeling about them or if he was just jealous.

He tossed a pile of advertising in the trash. A special deck of cards clanked in the can. They were mailed to churches offering everything to grow a church or to polish its image. He caught himself kicking the trash can under his desk a bit too hard. *Wonder if Rhonda heard that?*

And churches were no better, with their multi-million-dollar campaigns to build bigger and bigger buildings, huge campuses, and lofty reputations for their pastors. He must be jealous. Yes. No. Did it matter? He was done. Finished! He'd had it with this way of doing things; he was sick of hiding his true feelings for the sake of those selling the soul of the church.

The office telephone had rung continually since he arrived only a few minutes ago. There was a knock on his door. "Pastor Atkins?"

"Yes."

"Did you forget Ellen's surgery this morning?"

"Oh, no!" Trent grabbed the stack of calls to return, crushed them along with the conference ad, and chucked them into the trash can. He checked his pocket for his cell phone and flew out the door. *This is the day*, he thought. *Do I have the courage to run from all of this?* But another thought trumped this one. *Do I have the courage and stamina to stay?*

"Please know that I appreciate all you do here, Rhonda," Trent said as he headed out the door. Out of the corner of his eye, he saw her look up at him quizzically.

As he slipped into the front seat of his Jeep Cherokee,

Trent's cell phone rang. Looking out the window, Miss Simpson thought she saw him pound his fist into the steering wheel.

1:10 PM

The subway station was crowded. He wanted to be brash and shove people out of his way. But he also longed to comfort the homeless man begging in his path. Trent emptied his wallet into the beggar's cup, and turned away, fighting tears. *Why can't I change anything—or help anyone?*

He felt a mixture of relief and rage. He was making the boldest move of his life. Like a drowning man flailing for something to hold on to, for so long he had been grasping but couldn't hold on to anything. He had planned this for a long time. It made more sense than staying and imploding in his stress and rage.

A text message appeared on his cell. He read it. It was just another desperate soul who needed him to return a message wishing her peace and assuring her he'd pray. He took in a deep breath, said a prayer, and text messaged back. "Peace to you. I am praying." *What will they think when they know I've deserted?*

The first two bank machines were nearby. He withdrew the maximum. The next three were a block away. Did they have a way of monitoring these things? Would some sort of red flag be triggered? Stuffing the stack of twenties in his pockets, Trent headed back toward the transit station.

In his backpack, he had another envelope of money, cash collected secretly by pulling a dollar or two per week, sometimes more, out of his weekly allowance—unbeknownst to Natalie. Along with cash-laden handshakes after Christmas services, he had accumulated another two thousand dollars over the past two years.

Next, he found a park bench next to the canal. He called

his home phone, and left a message. "Natalie. I'm sorry things are always so hard. I'm sure I'll enjoy the conference, and will be in touch in a day or so. Enjoy the days with your mom."

Dialing another number, he called Jack Sprague, the most contentious member of the church elder board. He opted through to Jack's voice mail and said, "Hey, Jack. Sorry I won't be able to make tomorrow's lunch. I know you rarely agree with my decisions, but I'm making a big one today, and I think you'll love it. You'll hear about it Sunday." Applying all the pressure his thumb could muster, he pressed the end button.

He removed the SIM card and deleted all data from his cell phone. Then, certain no one was looking, Trent tossed the phone in the canal. He bent, bit, and twisted the SIM card, then tossed the pieces in two nearby trash cans. Already he was feeling lighter—although he had a nagging feeling that he should have made one more call to check back in with the office.

Grabbing a new prepaid cell phone from his backpack, he inputted a few numbers from a slip of paper, then crumpled and trashed it. He noticed a pink "while you were out" slip when he stuffed the phone away in his front pocket. Clenching his teeth, he scuttled the message without looking at it.

Then, taking the stairs down below the street, Trent stepped on an escalator and boarded another train. Sitting back, he studied the route map above the windows and counted the stations before the airport.

7:30 PM Central Time

Brandon Tyler and Natalie Atkins were the last to leave the worship band rehearsal. Having walked to the church building from her office, she needed a ride home, and he was more than willing to oblige. As they approached her house, she told him she had some of his favorite brownies if he wanted some.

Natalie had planned to invite Brandon in and was sure he would accept the invitation. But something funny happened as they pulled into the driveway. Natalie saw the bushes Trent had just trimmed, the flowers he had planted, and the hose that he never remembered to roll up. It was rolled up. She could not shake the thought of Trent. Even though she had dreamed of this evening for weeks, she could think only of her husband.

"Just sit tight, and I'll bring those out to you." She jumped from the passenger seat and punched the code into the garage door opener. Seconds later, she ran out with a plate loaded with brownies and covered in plastic wrap. She liked the way he looked at her as she bent over, leaning into the window of the car with the plate. "Got to run," she said as she bolted back into the house, a smile on her face.

Brandon's eyes followed her every move, and he wished she had invited him in.

Back in her house, Natalie grabbed the note she had hastily removed before delivering the brownies to Brandon. "Enjoy!" it said. She wrinkled her nose, embarrassed to see the heart she had drawn as the point below the exclamation mark. She would get her courage up tomorrow. Trent would only be gone for a few days.

She noticed her reflection in the entryway mirror. She was glowing, much like college girls she loved to tease when they were falling in love. The magic feelings faded quickly at that thought. Soon she felt tears in her eyes. *What is happening to me? What in the world am I thinking?*

—————— LIKE IT OR NOT ^{chapter 2}

7:30 PM Pacific Time

Trent found himself standing on a curb outside the airport looking over San Diego Harbor. Palm trees swaying in the California breeze made him smile. There were two bags and not a single regret on his shoulders—for now, anyway.

A taxi took him to an address on Point Loma. After pulling up to a beachfront property, he grabbed his bags and walked along a garden path banked by flower beds, into the front yard of an old friend. Chuck was sitting with a cup of iced tea, enjoying the cool evening breeze under the perfect sky. The house wasn't big, but Trent guessed the lot alone cost millions.

"Trent, my boy! Right on time." Chuck pulled another cup from behind him, dipped it into a cooler full of ice, and asked, "Tea or lemonade?"

"Lemonade sounds great, Chuck. Thanks."

They embraced, and Chuck, holding him at arm's length, asked, "So, how are you, friend?"

"Good, man." Trent sat down on a tropical-patterned lawn chair and let out a deep breath slowly, uncertainly. "I can't believe I'm here. Can't believe I'm doing this. Am I crazy, Chuck?"

"It could be, man. But I know what it's like to bail. And you've thought this through pretty well—and you've been thinking about it for quite a while." He paused, then looked Trent in the eyes and asked, "Seriously, how are you feeling?"

"Relieved, free, and maybe a little bit shell-shocked, you know?" Trent was looking mellow.

"Let's go catch the sunset. Grab your chair."

Early the next morning, Trent quietly got out of bed, made a pot of coffee, and took a cup of the steaming brew out on an upstairs deck. "God, have mercy on me, a sinner." Pause. "Lord Jesus Christ, Son of God, have mercy on me, a sinner." Another pause, a tear in his eye. Then, "Glory to you, Lord, glory to you."

And with that, he began and quickly finished his morning prayers.

Chuck had arranged the job weeks ago, and now Trent was riding to work in a pickup driven by Rico. It was still early on his first full day in the southwesternmost part of the United States. Today he and Rico would do demolition work inside what used to be a dentist's office, preparing the way for their company to rebuild it as an adult education center.

The hours went by quickly. Trent took no phone calls, received no messages, and didn't worry about anyone who was sick or depressed. He just ripped desks from walls—and walls from walls—and relished the simplicity of this hourly-wage job.

Having filled a second huge dumpster, he and Rico walked down the street to an In and Out restaurant for a burger, fries, and chocolate shake. The diet could wait! Besides, he had already lost fifteen pounds worrying over his decision the past few months. He and Rico were living big.

The radio blasted and a warm wind rushed through the pickup windows as Rico drove Trent back to Chuck's that evening. Trent was lost in his thoughts. He had escaped to Southern California, and he hoped he'd never be caught. Yet another part of him hoped he'd see Natalie waiting for him when they pulled up at Chuck's. But that wouldn't happen. He was sure his exit strategy was covert enough that she wouldn't find him, at least not for a long time. He wasn't sure she really wanted to find him anyway. They had drifted farther and farther apart for years. She had other things on her mind. He wondered if one of those things was a person.

Why had he done this irresponsible, unreasonable thing? Failure, of course: he had failed to develop a thriving marriage. Fatigue: he couldn't be a pastor any longer—there were too many hoops to jump through, too many people to please. Authenticity: he didn't believe in what his church had become and what he had become in its service. Continuing as a pastor would have been like a conscientious objector working in a munitions factory. Not a doubt in his mind—he was finished.

But couldn't he have found another, more reasonable way? Wasn't this mysterious escape of his rather melodramatic? Part of him wondered if he should run back home like a runaway child. But he'd gone far past the end of his driveway, and going back home to the life he'd left just yesterday didn't sound comforting at all. It sounded like prison.

He couldn't quiet his angry thoughts of Brandon Tyler. Even now, he could see Brandon in his mind. He dressed like a teenager, and his brownish blond hair fell in every direction, deliberately messy. His rounded nose and mischievous smile, along with his high eyebrows, gave him an almost elfin appearance. But he was handsome in a way that might be bad for his soul, and he certainly earned a few giggles from the teenage girls in their congregation.

Brandon was a good guy, really, Trent told himself. Sure, he could be a little sensitive about getting his own way, and sometimes his artiness clashed with Trent's eye for practicality. But Trent had hired him as the music minister because he liked him. Brandon thought outside of the typical church box and seemed to understand the style Trent had wanted for the Baylor's Bend worship services.

And he was an undeniably gifted musician. He led the worship band, and he and Natalie had played music together on Sundays for years. Last night, following practice, Brandon had probably given Nattie a ride home. A new thought struck Trent, one that had bubbled inside him but never surfaced: with him supposedly away at a conference for three nights, would Brandon and Natalie use the opportunity to spend time together?

He shook his head to clear his mind of self-flagellating thoughts and suspicions. Yes, when he was really honest with himself, Trent was concerned—very concerned—with the level of Natalie and Brandon's involvement. At one point he suspected a full-blown affair. But after watching and monitoring things for a couple months, he could find no evidence to support the sick feeling in the pit of his stomach.

He shook his head again and gave a small, pained smile. Even if there wasn't a physical affair, something emotional was going on between Natalie and Brandon. Was this the real reason he had run? Was everything else a smoke screen? He realized that with his absence, the very thing he dreaded— Natalie leaving him for Brandon—had become a much greater possibility. The distance that had widened between him and Natalie could now be counted in miles.

Trent confronted Natalie about Brandon only once. She protested vigorously and he ended up feeling like a creep. He did catch her in a lie, however, and several more after that. So while this trip might give her and Brandon the space they needed to act on their flirtation, something had been developing for most of the last year.

Funny, Trent thought. Natalie was back home lying to him, sure that *she* was the one with the big secret.

The sad thing was, after he got past the pangs of jealousy, he really didn't care what happened to the two of them anymore. He hadn't cared for quite a while, and neither had she. Maybe it was time to step out of the way of her happiness, which she might find with Brandon.

Yet everything about their work and life stood for something much different, much purer than brushed-aside wedding vows. As he thought over their past and the decisions they had made, he realized that he hadn't been enticed away by the allure or a new life or a new someone. The lie of their ministry had driven him away. Trent had long ago burned out and found his love for Christ sacrificed on the cross of busyness and success. Ministry had become just a job, something he'd never intended it to become.

He knew that Natalie had given up ever being his first love, certain his first love would always be serving and growing a church. Had he driven her to look for someone who treated her like a real person? Had Brandon merely picked up on her need? Trent felt sure about one thing: he was glad that their attempts at getting pregnant in order to strengthen their marriage had failed.

Trent knew what he was doing was wrong. But continuing with the lie seemed even worse. Natalie had been too proud to go to counseling with him, and they had been too busy to get help in any other way. And so now their emotional separation had been made physical. They were two thousand miles apart, and he didn't think they could ever be together again.

Late Thursday evening, Natalie realized something was amiss when she couldn't reach Trent on his cell phone. Her suspicion was confirmed when she got a call at home from Bishop Phillips's secretary. The Bishop had wanted her to check with Natalie and make sure everything was all right, since Trent had signed up for the conference but never arrived. She also wanted to know if he would want a refund or to transfer his tuition to a future event.

Where was he? Natalie wondered. Had he been in an accident? Or worse yet, was he hiding something from her? Someone? That was a strange thought, one she'd never entertained before.

On Friday morning, after another ten phone calls went straight to Trent's voice mail, Natalie tried calling her mother. "Mom, it's Nattie. Please call me back when you get this. Something weird is going on. It's with . . . oh, just call me soon. Please!" Was it time to call the police and file a missing person's report? To call hospitals and ask about accidents?

Later that morning, Trent's letter arrived at the bishop's office. Bishop Phillips took the opened letter from his secretary. She shook her head in disbelief and said, "This is going to be hard."

"What did you say?"

"Just read," she said and walked backward two steps so that she could watch the bishop as he read. She screened most of his letters for him, but this one was different from any other she had seen.

The letter told of Trent's plans to get lost, of his fears regarding Natalie and an affair. It spoke of sorrow and feelings of failure. It offered multiple apologies and reflected the soul of a broken man. The letter ended with these lines:

When I was very young, God called me to care for people. He invited me to be a part of giving to the poor and needy of the world. He gifted me with ability to explain Jesus to people who think they hate him. I was convinced that if our culture could truly hear about him, it would run to him. I still am convinced of that. I just don't believe they will ever run to the church as it is.

I couldn't face the fallout of what was coming in my marriage and of the results of my absolute failure at being a church CEO. All I could think of was to run. Enclosed please find my ordination credentials. You don't need to file them. I've known for years that once I left, I wouldn't need them again. You certainly don't need me on your team.

The bishop called Natalie. "Natalie, this is Bishop Phillips. Could my wife and I come over and meet with you?"

NEW WAYS

By the weekend Trent was breaking a bit. He began to remember weddings he'd promised to do "someday" for young girls without even a boyfriend; cases of cancer he'd begun but would not follow to the grave; babies he would not meet the day they were born; addicts who wouldn't know where to turn; the teenage girl who would think he'd left because she told him she was having an affair with a married man in the church; and the adolescent boy whose mom had taken up drinking again and was taking her drunken anger out on him.

He couldn't shake the memory of the widows who counted on his caring questions and the middle-aged man who had landed into life in a nursing home after a stroke crushed his mobility and speech. He wondered how his untrustworthiness would affect those who doubted they could trust in God. *Lord have mercy*, he often prayed.

Yet even though he deeply cared about his congregation, his vocational responsibilities had changed. He had become a CEO, a paper pusher, an arbiter between warring factions. His administrative team pushed him to record more hours on his weekly time audits. They didn't understand that all the hours between his official work were wearied with thoughts of arguments, of "a bone to pick with you" meetings, of concerns for people so lost in the tangles of life that they didn't know how to make it. They didn't know he had become a fundraiser, paying for an overdone church building while leaving the needy in the dust. They didn't know he couldn't smile anymore without a strained effort to perform—to make them feel good. They didn't understand that he loved ministry, but couldn't face his job anymore.

A Damien Rice tune welled up in his head: "I'm not God, I'm not God." They didn't know.

Trent ached over the knowledge that he had given up, that he was a quitter, and that many would suffer from his decision to run and hide. Few would understand. His actions were as selfish as suicide, but they left him alive. After all of the scheming he'd done—feeling like his back was against the wall, feeling desperate for some solution—quitting was the best he could come up with.

Monday morning, Trent's new boss, Nick, met him at the building entrance. "How do you like the work, Trent?"

"Great, I love it. I never knew you could get paid for tearing things up."

"I like your work. Let's talk Friday when you finish up here."

"You've got it."

Trent wondered about the purpose of the meeting, but figured it couldn't be bad. At the end of the day, he hopped a bus to the coast. Finding a public restroom, he ducked in, donned cut-offs, a T-shirt, and a pair of sandals, and stuffed his work clothes in his backpack. He walked along the sidewalk, dodging the occasional bike or rollerblader, until he came to a good place to park his towel.

Trent played with abandon in the water's brisk welcome. He even borrowed a boogie board from a kid who offered.

Sitting on the beach, he enjoyed the warmth of the sun, and soon put his T-shirt back on to avoid burning. The golfer tan would have to go, but it wouldn't all happen today.

The beach was busy, but the crowd didn't bother him. The voices and sounds gave Trent a feeling of belonging. A mother scolded her son for kicking sand on her towel, and just one blanket back, two teen girls gossiped about boys and teachers and favorite bands.

He realized something else, and the thought made him smile. No one knew him. The constant pressure to make appearances and perform was gone. So was the incessant anxiety-induced dizziness he had lived with over the past few years. One hope played in his mind as the sun warmed his skin: *resurrection.*

Arriving home that evening, Chuck met him at the front door, a knowing look in his eyes. "Which beach?"

"Del Mar," Trent said. "Beautiful. And the waves were awesome!" He paused. "Hey, Chuck. I need to find a permanent place to stay. But I have no clue where to look. Any ideas?"

"You know you're welcome here, man." But knowing Trent needed a place to settle into and consider home, he said, "There are a few Web sites and underground papers that list roommate needs. You might also check out the school up the coast, kids looking for roommates and all. Maybe you could fit in with one or two? And then there could be some rentals around that are right for a single. I'll keep my eye out."

"Thanks, Chuck. You know I appreciate the hospitality, but yeah, I've got to get a place before I chicken out and head home." Trent paused. He needed to unload, and the workout in the surf had worn at his resistance. Words tumbled from his mouth. "I'm being haunted—all my failures, all the people I've let down. I'm humiliated, and I feel I've cut every tie I've ever made." He wiped a tear. "I am so lost, Chuck."

"Let's talk, man. You need to let this out. Do you want me to call someone else?"

"No, Chuck. I decided a long time ago that if I ever came this far, I would stick it out. And I have no life to return to now anyway. I've already cashed it in. It's gone, Chuck. The old life is gone." And with that Trent headed to his room upstairs, hoping his friend didn't see his face twisting into a show of agony. Closing the door behind him and holding two pillows to his face, he sobbed out his sorrow.

Friday after work, Nick took Trent home to change, then out to dinner. They sat down at their table, ready to start the weekend. "Listen, Trent," Nick began, setting down his menu. He was a workout addict, and he had the build to show for it. Yet he carried himself with a kindness that fit his penetrating brown eyes and his caring smile. "We don't find hard workers like you every day. You look good, show up on time, speak Spanish, and have a great attitude. Frankly, you're what we look for. Chuck did us a huge favor when he sent you our way."

"Thanks, Nick. But really, I've never had such fun at a job before. Tearing stuff up, eating burgers and fries every day, then going to beach at night—this is like a vacation."

"We know keeping a guy like you isn't easy, so here it is. You are on track for supervisor if you want it. And whether you want it or not, the boss says we can bump you to over twenty bucks an hour right now. *And* after a few more weeks, I can increase that and get you a company truck and some on-time bonuses. Bottom line: we're benefiting from your skills, and we want to keep you."

Trent grinned and said, "I don't know what to say. Thanks! And I'll think about the supervisor thing. I mean, responsibility for anyone besides me is not what I came here looking for, but give me a few weeks, and we'll see."

"What else do you need, dude? Do you have a place to

stay? Do you need to know where the hot spots are for night life? Tell me, what do you need?"

"I don't know that either, Nick. I'm making the transition from Midwestern suit-man to California guy. I just need to find my way. And yeah, I could use a heads-up on any housing options you come across. I need to get out of Chuck's place, although he says I'm welcome. I just want to get my own life, you know?"

As he heard the last words, they sounded like they were spoken by a different person. They couldn't be his own. Was he really starting over completely? Permanently? Trent felt a lump catching in his throat and feared he might crash again and break down in tears. He was like a hormone-crazy teen girl or something. Why was he such a wimp? He gained control of the threatening emotions as he and Nick left the restaurant and walked out to Nick's work truck.

"Hey, I've got an idea," Nick said as he started the engine. "My parents have a place on Ocean Beach. It's a cool little apartment-bungalow-type place across from their pool behind the house. They don't need a renter, and hate the risks and hassle, so they don't rent it. But now and then they tell me to let them know if I meet someone who might need the place. A trustworthy guy could give them some added security, since they're on the beach. They would treat you fairly on the price."

"Uh, well, sure, Nick. Let me know if they're interested. I'd love to take a look. You know my income level." He grinned, thinking of the California rental rates and the impossibility of even dreaming about a beach rental.

Nick changed lanes suddenly, and made a right turn at a sign that read "To the Beaches." "We're right in the neighborhood; let me drive you by." Trent couldn't believe his eyes when they pulled around the back side of Nick's parents' place. Palm trees leaned over an in ground pool. Across the pale green water, he saw a perfectly sized, tidily maintained bungalow, the surf pounding the sand just behind it. "That's it, dude. Not bad, huh? It's furnished too!"

Natalie sat by her telephone hoping for a call and monitored her e-mail for a note or even a clue. She was stunned. Church friends called and stopped by, but they could only shake their heads. They were hurt as much as she was shocked.

Her regret over the distance between her and Trent haunted her. She remembered the times when no words were exchanged between them throughout entire weeks—maybe months. She had sensed his rage, and she knew he sensed her broken heart. Yet they had stubbornly drudged on until there was no more rage or brokenness, until their marriage was only public acting and private resentment. She knew her heart was elsewhere. She now assumed Trent's was too.

Bishop Phillips had spoken with local and state law enforcement to no avail. This was a clear case of abandonment, they told him—not so unusual with men nearing middle age. He'd probably come back, but if not, he'd most likely reestablish contact sometime in the future.

That Sunday afternoon, Trent moved into his new place. His two travel bags didn't take long to move, and a couple of trips to a Target store filled out what little was lacking. Nick acted like a doting father making sure everything was just right. His mother and father, Herb and Dot Shoemaker, told Trent they were "just excited to have someone in the old place." And Trent could tell they felt good about the extra security of younger man around. Chuck was amazed at Trent's good fortune. *What a place!*

Once they left him, Trent pinched himself on the forearm. He pulled back the curtains covering the glass wall that separated him from the Pacific. Cranking open a window, he could hear the pounding of the surf. The curtains lifted with the ocean breeze. This was nice. Way nice.

Yet, with all of these blessings, Trent could only wonder about what had happened on the other side of the country that day. A church had heard that he was gone. The leaders couldn't have offered much explanation. He'd quit. They would replace him. It was just that simple. He could be replaced.

Had Nat even gone to the services? Did he even care? Of course he did. He tried not to think about it.

The sun had long ago fallen into the deep green sea, and Trent tossed and turned restlessly into the night. He knew someday soon he would enjoy the sound of surf outside his window, but tonight too many questions echoed through his mind. He finally drifted off to sleep, thinking that it had been a long time since he had missed church on a Sunday. Today was a nice break. Next week, maybe, he would find a service.

Dear church friends:

What I have done is inexcusable. There is no apology that can make this right. I have humiliated my wife and church family, and I have failed my God and calling. Asking for forgiveness would only further my selfish actions. I want to say that I do care about how this affects you, and I do hope you will soon have a new shepherd and leader and can return to some form of normalcy. I continue to seek help from the high and lofty one (Isaiah 57:15).

Trent

It was as good as he could do. He felt strange not putting "Pastor" before his name. He tucked the letter in an envelope and mailed it to a friend who had promised to forward his mail.

It would arrive later in the week at the office he had fled only eight mornings ago.

Bishop Phillips called Natalie each day to check on her. She had locked up the parsonage and moved in with her mother. As the bishop stepped through the door and handed his jacket to Natalie's mother, he could see in Natalie's face a growing discomfort and confusion. He dreaded telling her about the new letter.

After listening, she asked where the letter had come from.

"Alabama" he said.

"From whom? What town?"

"No return address, Natalie. I'm sorry."

She sat sobbing, shaking her head, even as it rested in her hands. Suddenly she looked up. "But what about the postmark? Where is the postmark from?"

The Bishop opened his briefcase and pulled out the letter. "Hold on, I'll have a look."

Natalie read the faded mark. "Foley, Alabama. I've never heard of it." Stepping to the computer in her mother's den, she opened Mapquest and entered Foley's Zip code from the envelope. A second later a map appeared on the screen. "It's on the coast, near Gulf Shores. Gulf Shores! That's where his study group retreated a couple of years ago! He *has* been there. He must be there right now! How can I find him? I need to talk to him, I have to!"

Nick's parents had invited Trent, Nick, and Nick's new wife, Allie, to dinner on the Tuesday evening after he moved in. They were to grill steaks by the pool. Trent stopped on his way home from work and bought Mrs. Shoemaker a bouquet of flowers and a pound of baked beans from a deli. Once home, he found his nice pair of jeans and was surprised to find they were fitting him much better.

Pulling out a shirt, he remembered Natalie buying it for him. He hadn't liked it at first—the Hawaiian print seemed too flowery. But the more he'd worn it and gotten compliments on it, the more he grew to like it. It felt like a good friend by now.

And as he remembered Nat, he had another strange feeling. Trent remembered her smile, their first dates walking downtown near the seminary, holding hands and window shopping for hours at a time. Oh, how he had loved her. She was short and trim but shapely. Her dishwater blond hair, usually pulled into a ponytail, framed her freckled face and green eyes. He feared her eyes were worried tonight. Sitting there, in his flowered shirt, Trent allowed himself to really think of her for the first time since he left. He had avoided her memory with all of the energy he had for the past week and a half. When tempted to think of her, he would shove the thoughts aside with dark ones of envy and spite, imagining her cheating heart.

But in these moments, he realized that he was burying a deeper truth: long before he'd sold out on ministry, he had sold out on her. Trent had given up hope and decided he would woo her no more. He was a loser. Why not lose his wife and her love for him while losing his career?

He had forty-five minutes before the gathering, so he shuffled down to the beach for a walk. He grabbed a handful of Kleenex, in case the choking tears couldn't be kept inside amidst the gulls' cries.

Frank Sinatra crooned from hidden speakers in the garden surrounding the pool. Herb was preparing a skillet of mushrooms in butter next to the sizzling steaks. Dot was fawning over the flowers Trent gave her and moving about the patio in step to the music. The ocean breeze was gentle, and the night was warm, but cooling quickly.

"Herb, honey, could you carry these glasses to the table when you get a second?" Dot asked.

"I've got them." Trent grabbed the festive-looking stemware two at a time, and carried them to their places beside plates and salad bowls. "Need me to grab these napkins too?"

"Oh, you're such a dear. Would you?"

It wasn't until the silver was wrapped and in place, the table set to perfection with a candle burning behind the protection of a glass globe, that Trent noticed that six places were set. Before he could wonder, he heard Nick approaching.

"Hey, Trent! Dude, did Mom put you to work?" Nick was hugging his mother while holding a bottle of wine in each hand. "She's really pretty easy to work for," he said, smiling at his mom.

Trent's head began to swim as he processed the extra place setting, the bottles of wine, and a beautiful dark-eyed beauty walking around the pool with Nick's wife.

"Trent, this is my wife, Allie. I think you saw her at the site yesterday. And this—" he paused for effect, "—is Kim, a really good friend of Allie's." Then, whispering into Trent's ear, he said, "Don't worry, dude, she's cool."

Nick wasn't sure if that meant she was taken, not interested, or what. He did know there wasn't room for romance at this point in his recovery, and Kim was a knockout. He was also feeling the weight of his innocence. He had never had more wine than the sip he got at some communion services. His church was tea totally. He wasn't sure he knew how to live in this new world.

Dinner ended with a stroll down to the beach. The men walked together, as did the women. Nick explained to Trent about Kim. Her husband had died in a car crash just a year and a half ago. She didn't come with any expectations. She was just trying to get back out among people. Allie had invited her to come along, thinking that "gentle Trent," as Nick had described him, might be a decent date for her someday.

Bonfires twinkled up and down the coast. Trent had just begun hoping his party might start one of their own when Dot announced, "Here we are." And pulling a lighter out of her bag, she set fire to a pile of driftwood Herb had built earlier. Chairs sat around the wood in a ring, and everyone took a seat. Trent sat between Herb and Allie, with Kim opposite him.

The next two hours were spent in wonderful human friendship. Kim was able to tell her story. Her eyes told a tale of sadness—and of growing hope. And as the group listened, she seemed comforted. Trent couldn't help but think of the wonderful intimacy of fellowship he'd enjoyed in church small groups.

Dot told of the great relief just last month when a lump turned out to be benign. Herb moved his chair closer to hers, put his hand on her leg, and smiled. Nick told the circle how grateful he was for Trent's contribution to his business. Then, turning to Trent, he said, "So, Trent. We know very little about you, dude. Where are you from?"

"Just south of Chicago. Moved out here because I needed a change. Needed some perspective. I'd rather not give many details. Let's just say, life couldn't go on as it was, and I needed a clean break. And as it turned out, my buddy Chuck knew Nick here, and the rest is history." He was relieved when his story was accepted without any follow-up.

For the next several minutes, very few words were spoken. The flicker of hot coals, the gentle roar of the flames, and the crashing of the surf were all the moonlit night needed. Trent thought of how sweet it was to be simply one of a crowd.

35

To *not* be special was so special. No one expected him to be profound or offer some insightful comment about what a blessing these friendships were. No one asked him to pray or advise. He could just be blessed by their company, and blessedly common.

He pulled the hood up on his sweatshirt, closed his eyes, and leaned back into his chair. Even though he knew he wouldn't, he wanted to talk. He wanted to tell these new friends about Natalie. They would have liked her. He wanted to call her. But that was not in the plan. When he got back to the privacy of his bungalow, he would write her a note of apology, and send it to Alabama to be forwarded on.

Hide and Seek

Bishop Phillips promised Natalie he would do some homework. He started by contacting the bishop for the Coastal Alabama area, armed with only a few clues. Trent had gone with several northeastern Illinois pastors on a study retreat to Gulf Shores last year, and they'd stayed in a timeshare owned by one of their congregants. Bishop Phillips asked the bishop there to call around to the local pastors and see if they had any recollection of this group. Did any of them know Trent Atkins? Had they seen him? Alabama's Bishop Alders said he would do his best and call back soon.

Meanwhile, Natalie was making plans of her own. She convinced her mother to make a road trip to Foley, Alabama. She knew Trent pretty well. And she had some good ideas of where to look for him. She wanted to catch him with whoever it was. She needed to prove *she* was the one cheated.

> *Nattie,*
>
> *Just wanted to let you know I am well. Nat, I have been such a loser and a failure. I'm sorry I let you down so horribly. You deserve better. Maybe someday I will be able to face you again, but for now, I must be*

*away. Take all the stuff. Give this note to any attorney
or whoever. I'm starting over, and maybe I won't blow
my life—and the lives of innocent others—so badly
this time. Sorry I've made you miserable for so long.*

Trent

Trent thought of Brandon as he wrote the note. Why
had he let that punk win his Natalie? But then he paused—
underneath that thought was another one. Why had he ever let
their love die? This was his fault.

After addressing the envelope to Alabama, he was
heading for bed when he saw a folded piece of paper on the
floor near the door. He opened the note and read: "I'd like
to chat sometime. Kim—619-555-8921. No big deal if you'd
rather not."

As Trent held the slip of paper, he was seeing her
beauty. He didn't recall having studied Kim well enough to
be remembering the details now flooding his mind. Her eyes
were innocent, yet seductive. She was petite, while her blue
jeans and modest knit top accented a shape he struggled now
to shake from his mind.

Yet far beyond all of her physical attributes, he
remembered sensing a deeper treasure in this woman. She
possessed a certain grace and compassion in the way she
carried herself, and her caring gaze focused on people as they
told their stories. It was like she knew who she was and knew
what really mattered—she knew that people mattered. Kim
had experienced a baptism of pain, and she'd emerged soaked
in authenticity.

Before he could think, he reached for the phone.

Natalie hung the last of the clothing she had packed, and then
left her mom, Emma, to rest at the hotel. The daylong ride to
Gulf Shores had been full of speculation of Trent's affair. "I'll

bet he's been communicating with her since he came last year. We sure haven't communicated," she said to her mother.

Even though it was evening, there were still two contacts she wanted to try tonight. It was Wednesday, and a couple of the churches in town, places Trent might have visited, might be open for services.

"No, don't recall seeing him. Sorry you're having such trouble, ma'am," the older gentleman said in his Southern drawl. His wife gave Natalie a look of sympathy.

Natalie was questioning some of the parishioners before speaking with the pastor, just in case he was sworn to some sort of secrecy. But the crowd was thinning, as were her opportunities.

"Pastor Collins, I was wondering if I could interrupt you for a moment." She held out a picture of Trent. "This must sound crazy, but my husband is a pastor too, and I have reason to believe he is in the area. I think something may be wrong with him."

James Collins looked at the picture for a moment and said, "No, I'm sorry, I don't recognize him. Have you called the police or sheriff's office?" He paused. "Did you say he's from the area?"

"No, no. I just have reason to believe he came here, and maybe something happened to him, or maybe. . . ." Her voice broke off.

"Now, now. Don't you worry none." He was patting her on the shoulder. "I'm sure he's just fine."

After she spent the entire evening at this church, she found the other one closed up when she drove by. She would start fresh in the morning. She had breakfast scheduled with Bishop Alders at 7:00 AM sharp.

That night in the hotel, Natalie could not help but reflect on

39

the better days her marriage had known. She could have confronted Trent countless times when he was absent—absent while still in the house. But they both had thrived on barriers, and now they were paying the price. At least she hoped they both were—she hoped Trent was as miserable as she was.

Yet there was Brandon. She knew Trent had seen the subtle touches between them. He'd mentioned it one time, and she thought she had covered well. It had been such a tough load to bear, caring for Brandon while keeping the emotional sparks from becoming a fire. Now, at least, she had the hopes that she and Brandon might be able to move past the longing glances and the subtle phone messages and e-mails.

She had always managed to do the expected, to keep up appearances for the congregation. Now Trent had blown that sky high. Appearances! What fools they must look like to their parishioners.

The plan was to meet Kim in Old Town San Diego. He went out and bought a pair of shorts and a new shirt. He wore his favorite shirt the night he'd met Kim, and although he didn't mind wearing the same outfit a few days in a row, it just didn't seem like such a good idea to be dressed the same as the night they'd met.

A row of guys sitting at outdoor tables ogled Kim as she past them. One of them winked at Trent. But this was just a friendship thing, not a date at all. *Right*, he thought to himself. *I always go out to nice restaurants with beautiful women I'm counseling.* But no matter how much he had told himself that the old life was gone, it was not. He was a married man, and this felt like cheating. And he was miserable for it. His charm fought through, though. He was, after all, a pro at acting happy when his world was falling apart.

Kim was charming as well. She was not flirty. They were just having a nice chat, and from all appearances, she seemed to be enjoying herself.

Reverend Bob Strunk arrived at his office early on Thursday morning. Motivated to finish his sermon so he could take his Friday off, he headed straight for his commentaries. A stack of mail was sitting next to the "while you were out" slips. The letter on top caught his eye. It was another letter from Trent.

"Oh, shoot!" he said aloud to himself. He was tired of this game. He thought he knew Trent Atkins, and now he was wondering if he was some kind of criminal. Why all the secrecy? Why the cloak-and-dagger behavior? He thought of calling Bishop Alders, but was embarrassed to admit he'd agreed to such a scheme in the first place.

He picked up his phone and dialed Pastor James Collins from Seaside. "James. How are you?"

"Good, Bob. How've you been?"

"Good. Yes, I'm good too. Hey, James, I've got a crazy situation here, and I was wondering if I could pick your brain for a minute?"

"Sure. Fire away!"

"Did I ever mention the group of pastors that came here on some kind of a retreat last year? They stayed in a condo down at the tennis resort."

"No, Bob, I don't believe you did."

"Well, they were from Illinois, not far from Chicago somewhere. And they just came down together to enjoy a timeshare someone had given them, and to do some studying and have some fun. Well, I got to know one of them fairly well. Good guy and all, just . . . well . . . different."

"How do you mean, Bob?"

"He asked me to do something for him. Said he was going to be on a trip and needed to keep his whereabouts a secret from some folks back home. Said they wouldn't understand until some time later when he'd fill them in." He

41

paused. "James, you with me so far?"

"Keep going."

"Well, he said he needed to send mail to me and have me forward it for him. He wanted the postmark to be from Alabama so they wouldn't catch on to the surprise. Something about getting a place ready for his wife, and she wouldn't know what he was doing, because the letters came from here and all—you know? He said it would only be for a few weeks. *Then,* he'd send her tickets and show her a place he'd inherited where they could retire someday and vacation in the meantime."

"Yeah?" James asked.

"Well, he's been sending letters. And I've been forwarding them. And now it seems weird. Like, what if this guy is a conman or something?"

"Hmm. What's your gut tell you?"

"To call you and see what your gut says." They both chuckled.

"This guy was a pastor?" James asked.

"Yes."

"Oh, my Lord!" The color bled from James's face. "Was his name Trent . . . something?"

"Yeah, James. How did you know?"

Kim and Trent had decided to take a walk together on the beach by Trent's place the next night after work and a quick dinner. Thursday evenings were boneless wings night at a local eatery. They grabbed a dozen and then rode together to Trent's place, where they accessed the beach.

Trent sat facing Kim on a blanket. They ate wings and drank sodas as the breeze played in their hair and the world stayed somewhere else. The sun was well above the horizon when they began their walk, and it had set long before they got back to the car. She told her story again, and Trent listened well. He told her of his marriage that had grown cold, but managed to change the subject when she asked about his line of work back east.

A couple of times throughout the evening, she leaned in toward him as they walked. He knew he could have taken her hand or put his arm around her shoulder, and truthfully, he wanted to. An addiction to morality, maybe—he was just not able. However, his reluctance to take this simple step seemed to make Kim more interested.

Trent had a lot to think about. Clearly, this was not the right path. Forget morality. Even if he were just some common Joe and not a pastor, running away from home and starting a relationship two weeks later was simply not healthy. No, he had to back away. He would tell her at the coffee date they had set for Friday.

After Pastor Strunk called, the bishop immediately called Natalie to his office. He told her that her husband was sending messages from Southern California to Illinois, via Alabama. The relay person was indeed a pastor, who thought he was helping with a great surprise—for Natalie herself. "He thought your husband was planning a surprise for you," he explained softly.

Her mother held her hand as Bishop Alders shared the bad news. Then Natalie heard him begin to weave hope into the story. "Our letters all have postmarks, and from that, perhaps we can take another step. In fact, I have contacted Bishop Jantzen at our Southern California, San Diego office." He paused and let out a deep breath. "Maybe we can trace Trent to a visit in one of our churches there."

"Or maybe there's some person in Southern California who's forwarding the letters from Mexico or something!" Natalie's countenance fell as she settled into the reality that Trent was lost. And he was lost on purpose.

43

"I'll let you know if I find anything, honey. I'll keep in touch. In the meantime, hang on to hope. And don't stop praying."

How many times had she heard Trent sweet-talk others in the face of disaster? The thing was, Trent really did care deeply—too deeply. She had tried to get him to let go a bit, draw a line for his emotions. And as they had been warned, he burned out. He had run from her emotionally, then the church spiritually, and now both physically. There were more than miles between them now.

"God be with him," she heard the bishop say into her thoughts from some distant place.

Trent and his crew had pulled twelve-hour shifts Monday through Thursday, pushing a project to completion. And when Nick drove up at 7:00 Friday morning, he was buoyant. "I wanted you to do this walk-through with me, Trent. You learn the art of bidding, and what you are about to do—the walk-through—and you can manage for us."

"Thanks, Nick. I've enjoyed myself. I'm getting in shape, and I love the variety." Trent pulled at the loose waistline of his jeans and smiled. "Bet I've lost fifteen pounds."

Tying their meetings up by 11:00 that morning, they drove back to Trent's. "We're pleased, dude. Really love your work." He handed him an envelope. "You've got the rest of the weekend off, and this is a bonus for finishing early and well." Nick was glowing. "You made us a bundle hitting this early bonus date."

Trent took the envelope and shoved it in the back pocket of his jeans. "Thanks, Nick."

"Trent, we're meeting with the boss first thing Monday morning. That, dude, can only mean good things."

"Natalie. We have sent Trent's picture to Bishop Jantzen." It was Bishop Phillips. "He has promised to send it to all of his congregations. If Trent has shown up in any of their churches, they will most likely recognize him. Now all we can do is wait and pray."

She found herself wondering if she wanted to know. Brandon was sending stronger signals, even stopping by the office to see how she was doing. Maybe she was ready for a new day. In that case, some unexpected repentance from Trent might ruin it.

chapter 5
TRUE COLORS

D ark clouds hung over the Pacific and a strong breeze
pushed them toward the coast. The sunshine on the
veranda wasn't likely to last through the afternoon.

Kim had recommended the trendy bistro which sat
across the street from the beach, only a few miles from Trent's
place. As he sat across from her and drummed his fingers on
the table, he noticed just how little he wanted to step away
from this new friendship. Perhaps he should just tell her he
wanted to go slowly.

They had just ordered their lunch and handed their
menus to the waiter when a commotion broke out on the street
below them. The sound of a woman screaming rose above
the surf's crashing. Before Kim could ask Trent what was
happening, he was running downstairs and then toward the
street.

Lying between two cars parked along the curb, the
severely overweight woman was in a full-scale panic attack.
Her foot was turned around one hundred and eighty degrees
and backward—her ankle had snapped as she miss-stepped on
the curb. Several bystanders looked on helplessly.

As Kim approached the car, she could see Trent, on one

knee, holding the woman's hand. His other hand stroked tears from her face. He was speaking to her, no sign of alarm in his voice. It was if he was smiling a kind, gentle strength into her psyche.

"Peace, my friend. You will be OK. I promise. All will be well. Peace."

Hearing those words and sensing some deep calm in Trent, she relaxed and relinquished herself to the pavement until help could arrive. "Who are you?" she asked through a newly peaceful smile.

"Your friend. Just a friend who cares for you."

As the stretcher was pulled from the emergency wagon, Kim heard Trent saying—no, it was as if he were *singing*—to this audience of one: "You are a unique, unrepeatable miracle of God. And he loves you just the way you are."

"Thank you" she breathed, tears coming again to her eyes. "I'll try to believe that."

"What is your name?"

"Carmen."

"Believe it, Carmen. You are his loved child, the target of his adoration." He released her hand as the medics stepped near.

As the ambulance pulled away, the bystanders lingered quietly, circled around where Trent sat cross-legged on the curb. It was as if they were awaiting instructions, or maybe a speech.

Finally, a young surfer in nothing but board shorts broke the silence. "Dude! Are you a healer or a yogi or something?"

Trent continued to sit quietly on the curb. He was oblivious to those who had gathered to watch him. He was looking at the small amount of blood on the pavement. It looked like he might be praying.

Moments later, those who had gathered slowly

dispersed, and Trent stood and stared at the sea.

"Trent?" Kim took him by the arm. "Who are you? What are you?"

"I don't know," he whispered, still looking out to sea. "I don't know." A light rain began to fall as they returned to their lunch, neither as interested in food as they had been thirty minutes earlier. As they walked to their cars, he assured her he'd call soon. Trent's mind was stuck on the question she had asked; her mind was stuck on his answer.

The hospital was just up the freeway. He'd done this a thousand times before. "Yes, my name is Trent. A young woman named Carmen was just in an accident up the coast. Um, I was there and wanted to see if I could check on her."

"I'm sorry sir, but—"

"I'm a pastor. Please, just let me just make sure she's OK."

The nurse led him past several curtained rooms. Finally she stopped, and checking the number hanging from the ceiling, she said, "21E. This is it."

Three hours later he met with Carmen's mother and a surgeon as she explained the procedure Carmen's ankle would need. Before the operation, Trent held hands with Carmen and her mother and prayed, giving thanks for the medical treatment and asking for a blessing on all of the professionals who would work on her ankle. Two and a half hours later, he accompanied Mrs. Perez to meet the surgeon in a family consultation room. There she pronounced the surgery a success. She said Carmen would need to stay overnight and would require weeks of physical therapy, but would be able to leave—with a wheelchair—first thing in the morning.

Trent exchanged numbers with Rosario Perez, and assured her that if either she or her daughter needed anything, he would be glad to help out. "Thank you, Pastor Trent," she said. Had he told her? It didn't matter. As he walked through the starry night on wet pavement, he deeply breathed in the joy of caring for this needy family.

Back at his home, he noticed the message light blinking on the telephone. "Hi, Trent. Could you give me a call when you get in tonight? I'll be up late. I just need to ask you a question." It was Kim.

He wasn't sure he wanted to add anything complicated to the night. Giving spiritual and emotional care could drain him. But he did feel the need to talk a bit.

"Kim, it's me, Trent."

"Hey, thanks for calling back. I was just hoping to talk with you. You have a few minutes?" Quiet. "Or, really, if this is a bad time. . . . "

"No, Kim, this is good. I could use a little conversation right now. Would you like to meet me for a walk?"

"Now? Sure, yes. Where?"

"I'll pick you up."

Kim ran out to the truck with two beach chairs in her arm. She was wearing blue jeans and a gray UCSD hooded sweatshirt. Her brown eyes sparkled with excitement as if she were fifteen years younger and sneaking out of her parent's home. "I'll just throw these in the back."

As she jumped in the truck, she put her hand on Trent's shoulder. "So, how was the rest of your day?"

Trent was caught up in thoughts of what he was doing. He was sitting alone in a vehicle with another woman for the first time in a decade and a half. His heart was racing with excitement and condemning him all at the same time. "What? I'm sorry, what did you say? I was preoccupied with, um, you." Did he really say that?

Kim blushed. "How was your day, after our weird lunch?"

"It was good, Kim. Really good."

The rain earlier in the day had made for few beachcombers that night. Kim led Trent to a favorite spot along the coastal highway. He grabbed the beach chairs and they waded through the wet sand toward the breaker line. Placing them just outside of the reach of the strongest waves, they dug their chairs in and sat down.

"Whoa, this is nice," Trent said.

"Mm-hmm."

Silence. Trent wondered if he should say something. It was usually his role to break silence. He peeked at Kim to see if she was feeling awkward in the quiet. But she had leaned back, her eyes closed, and she was softly smiling into the moonlight. No pressure here. He did the same.

After a few moments, Kim asked, "Trent, can I tell you some more about my marriage and the past year and a half?"

"Of course, Kim. Seems like a good place to empty a heart. Maybe the breakers can wash the bad stuff out."

Kim wove stories of grief, agony, and newly ascending hopes into the night. Her husband had been a hurting man. He had found it difficult to commit to Kim in the first place. Then, after they got married, his feelings of inadequacy had driven him to addiction. His doctors had been far too accommodating about refilling painkiller prescriptions. He'd gotten lost in them, and she had become lost to him. Though her husband had been dead just under eighteen months now, she had been alone for years.

But loneliness was something she'd always known. Her parents were both career driven, and she—an only child—had spent much of her young childhood alone or combing the beach with friends from school. She had done her share of partying and gotten bored with that. She had only wanted to have a family, a husband who loved her and children to whom she could give herself.

When her story was done, she got quiet, perhaps allowing the breakers to carry the pain away. She felt odd not needing to apologize for dumping her feelings out on him or for taking up his time. She knew she'd spoken to someone who cared.

Trent was thinking something similar. He felt no need to speak words of comfort. His silence seemed to be the more adequate gift.

Seagulls shrieked as they swooped past, hoping for a handout. Couples drifted along, arm in arm, and occasionally packs of youth would go by, making more noise than the evening called for, as was true to form. Between waves, a boom box from up the beach could be heard playing jazz.

Fifteen minutes must have passed before they spoke again. "You were wonderful with that woman today, Trent."

"Thanks."

"No, I mean, you were amazing. She went from spastic to peaceful in your hands. It was like you knew her, who she was and what she needed." She looked at Trent. "It was as if you really cared, really . . . loved her."

"I guess I did. I mean, I do."

"What do you mean? Have you met her before?"

"No. It was just that she needed loving. She needed to be cared for. She needed to know that she is incredibly important and wonderful." His eyes were glistening. "She just needed to know that."

"Yeah, I guess she did. But no one else spoke that stuff to her. No one else would think of it. It was just weird to see. Wonderfully weird, but weird. It was like love just overflowed out of the Pacific, splashed on you, and poured out on her. Love and hope and, I don't know—courage. Yes, courage."

He didn't know what to say. "Just like peace and calm are beaming from that moon, off of your face, and into my soul," he said, looking at her, their chairs a *v* pointing to the sea. "You are just what I need right now. Thank you."

"Trent, are you a religious person?"

"Yeah. I am."

"Talk to me about your faith, Trent."

She followed his eyes as he looked out over the sea toward the moon and the stars. "Love made all of this. Love so intense it reaches out to you and me and says, 'Love me back!' And I do. I love Love back. And Carmen—that woman we met today lying on the street—has been so unloved that Love begged me to love her. So I did."

"That's . . . that's beautiful. I think. Does this love have a name, or a religious circle where it hangs out?" Kim asked.

"I think Love's name is Jesus. And I'm not sure where He hangs out anymore."

"That's why I like being around you, Trent. You find the sore spot in me and make it better. Make it feel loved—I mean, not love like in the movies, but you make me feel as if I'm important. Like I'll be OK. Thanks for that."

A few moments passed.

"I have an aunt with cancer," Kim said. "Would you . . . could you go see her? She has gotten so sad and lonely. She needs to be loved, and we are all out of ways to tell her."

"Sure, I'd be happy to see her," he said. "What's her name?"

"Jo Anna. I think I'm learning the answer to my question, Trent. You know, the one I asked earlier today—'Who are you?'"

Trent could only think of how much he wanted to take Kim's hand in his. *Yet*, he thought, *if she only knew that this troubadour of God's love was flirting with adultery*. And she couldn't know that thoughts of Natalie were haunting him. "I'm not all as wonderful as you think, Kim. I'm just me, and it makes me happy to be with you right now."

She stood and moved her chair close to his. His heart pounded as she took his hand in hers and laid them on her lap. How could he be doing this?

chapter 6

——————— STEPPING OUT

Dear Natalie,

I don't deserve you. Consider me out of your life. Again, I relinquish my rights to any and all possessions. Please see Jim—he should be able to settle the legal aspects of this divorce as quickly as possible. Please forget we ever were. You need to know you are free. Please just forget me.

Trent

Even as he wrote the note, he felt the fault line dividing his soul. He wanted no part of the life he and Natalie had lived, and he figured it was too late for them anyway. But he didn't want to hurt her, and part of him wanted to have her back.

Another part of him wanted to start over as this new Trent on the west coast, the guy who lived in the beachside bungalow and dated the beautiful, dark-eyed girl with the cheerleader figure. She needed him now. She thought he could love and heal her, put her back together. This was right!

But, he thought, *this is wrong.*

Placing the letter in the envelope, he doubted he would send it. But in a fit of determination, he sealed and stamped it and dropped it in the mailbox. There. Done. He was indeed running away.

It seemed like the right thing, the only thing. But his mind still ached with doubt. *What have I done?*

As he drove away from the postbox, Trent thought of pulling over to release the tears and agony that were welling up inside him. But he decided yet again to bury all thoughts of the past. He would completely put away his old life. It was finished. Let the new one begin. And this decision led him back to the question, "Who am I?"

Natalie could only worry about getting caught when Brandon proposed dinner and a movie. He was sure she was playing hard to get; really, she was scheming to think of a way they could get together without being seen.

Brandon was a lifelong churchman. His faith had been sincere—or at least he never felt the need to question his devotion. He loved good music, and he loved making it happen. He enjoyed the spotlight, the satisfaction of knowing that his abilities impressed his listeners. He loved the rush he felt when the crowds lifted their arms in praise and danced and swayed to his music. It was his calling—to lead people to God through worship.

He listened to Christian music only, nothing else, and he had whole shelves full of CDs by his favorite Christian bands and solo acts. He decorated his office walls with their posters and placed quotes from their songs around his apartment. He was good at mimicking their sounds and styles and performing their music, and his renditions of songs by top Christian acts continually amazed the people at Baylor's Bend.

It never dawned on Brandon that calling a Christian concert a "show" might be contradictory, that church music should serve a different function than impressing the listener. Pop Christian music culture flowed through his veins, and he

56

loved it. Benny, a friend who deejayed at the local Christian radio station, had always told Brandon it was just a matter of time before his stuff would make it big. He knew some names in the business, and a big label was bound to sign him someday. More and more, Natalie had become a part of that dream for Brandon, and as things developed, he believed their big break was coming. He could think of little else. Trent had always complimented Brandon's strong self-motivation. Brandon didn't like waiting for anything, and in the case of Natalie, he was obsessed.

Trent stopped by the hospital to see Carmen and Rosario before they went home. Rosario asked which church he served as pastor. He told her he was a pastor with no church, prayed with them, and drove back to his beachfront bungalow for a day of rest.

On Sunday morning, Trent shuffled through the yellow pages, looking at the hundreds of worship opportunities up and down the coast. He went to the heading for his own denomination and grimaced as he envisioned the hustle of last-minute preparations happening at each church. He felt tired already. Closing the huge volume, he decided to walk up the beach to a worship service of a different denomination altogether—the church of sun and sky. He didn't want to risk seeing anyone he knew, or even any literature that looked familiar.

She pulled her phone from her purse, trying to answer it in time. "Hello, this is Natalie."

"Natalie. It's Brandon. I was wondering if you've heard anymore from the bishop."

"No. I mean, he calls every couple of days, but nothing has changed. California is a black hole. He's gone, Brandon! He hasn't even written any more notes or letters. He's left me.

57

I think I'd rather hear that he has died!"

"I doubt that, Nat. You're bound to be angry. It's part of grief. It's part of getting back to normal. But you will, Nat. You will get back normal."

No response. She was further along than he thought. Brandon didn't fully realize that she had been in the process of detaching for years. It was as if the love she and Trent had shared became void of any hope or joy. Like an old balloon, their relationship had slowly leaked out all the air, and it was dull and shriveled.

"Hey, I have your plate. You know, the one you gave me with the brownies? I'd like to get it back to you, and since you haven't been back at church, well, I wondered if I could run it by your office or your mom's house?"

"Could you stop by the office today? Around lunch? I'd love to talk to someone less stuffy than a bishop."

When Brandon arrived at the office, Natalie was not at her desk. A coworker gestured to a closed door across the hallway. Brandon peered into the conference room through a glass door to see her speaking with Bishop Phillips. She was holding a Kleenex box on her lap.

Thinking it was better if the bishop didn't see him, he borrowed a pen and paper from Natalie's coworker and wrote a note.

> *Hey Nat,*
> *I saw you with Bishop Phillips. Didn't want to disturb you. Please call if I can help.*
> *Brandon.*

He folded the note and taped it to the top of her plate, then sat it on her desk. Returning the pen, he told the woman to be sure to encourage Natalie to call if she needed a friend.

"She's a wonderful girl," he said as he stepped away.

Monday morning, Trent called Kim's apartment while she was at work. "Kim, thanks for the time at the beach Friday night. You will never know how much that time meant to me. I have to be away this weekend, but if we could have dinner some evening this week, I'd love it. How about tomorrow, 7:30, at Trevoli's? Let me know. Oh, and I'd be happy to go see your aunt."

Trent knew he needed some time away, so he'd called a monastery and made reservations for a silent retreat the next Friday evening through Sunday. Now he just had to make it through the week. He had to establish some ground rules, some personal guidelines, for the next chapter of his life. True, he would no longer be a pastor. But the dramatic shift his life had taken demanded that he settle himself into some workable person. He wanted things to be new. But he had to stay true to whatever remained of his old shattered image.

Natalie dialed Brandon's cell phone. "Could you see me? I'm taking the rest of the day off."

"Be right there."

Brandon took Natalie to the city. She told him her story as they sat in the playground swings of a park. She spoke of Trent, a man she had once loved. Yet, she told Brandon, that love had died long ago. Then, throwing caution to the wind, she said, "I want to be free and be yours. But Trent's disappearance leaves me hanging. What would people think?

"When he disappeared, Brandon, it was like the game was over. Reality snapped into sharp focus, and I realized that the excitement of toying with this affair had become as real as concrete." She paused and looked straight at Brandon. "I think he knew about our feelings.

"And I've known Trent hated his job for a long time. He

felt like he had sold out to large church ministry. He could no longer use his gifts of loving people and being with them. 'I've turned into a CEO.' I can hear him saying it now. 'All I do is raise money, hold meetings, and sit in my office.'

"But there's more to it, Brandon. Trent stayed with his job because I wanted him to. And he thought you and I were more than, well, what we've been. At one point, he thought we were having a full-blown affair. Of course I told him there was nothing going on at all, but he still had some suspicions about our closeness. And I think that when he believed he'd driven me toward you, he had nothing left to stay for."

"Can I say something here?" Brandon asked.

"Sure."

"We wanted so badly to get together. But we knew how wrong it would look to our families. I would lose my job, and you would lose the respect of all those around you."

"Yeah?" She looked at him.

"Don't you see it, Natalie?" He said. "Now we can have our cake—each other, that is—*and* our reputations. I can hear them now. 'That poor girl, left behind in such a horrible way. But now she's putting it all back together again. It's just like she and Brandon were meant for each other.' Natalie, we are home free.

"We just need to keep this a secret for several months, or a year, or whatever. Then we have a date and everyone is excited. Then we will be as natural and obvious a match as any fairy tale couple has ever been!"

Natalie had tears in her eyes. She looked into the distance and said, "Yeah, beauty and the beast." And she let out a quick breath of laughter. Then, drawing in another, she became serious. "And sometimes fairy tales have bad endings."

Monday morning's meeting with the boss provided even more compliments and promises. Trent's salary was bumped yet another level, and now he received a percentage of any jobs he bid, oversaw, and finished. He had a work truck for business and personal use, and it even came with a gas card. The job was going well.

Even so, Tuesday seemed to drag on forever. He had scheduled a meeting with a customer for the end of the day, and as 6:45 came and went, the customer had not yet shown. Trent's 7:30 meeting with Kim was beginning to look impossible when suddenly the man drove up, announcing he'd lost track of time. "I'll have to come by tomorrow morning," he said.

Trent sprinted down the street to his truck, hoping he'd hit no traffic deadlocks. Once home, he showered and dressed and was back in his truck in less than fifteen minutes. Pulling into a parking spot just down from the restaurant, he walked up the sidewalk at 7:29.

Twenty minutes later, Kim came running to the entrance, looking frantically for him. "I'm so sorry! I got stuck in traffic and then I had to park about five blocks away." Trent smiled and opened Trevoli's front door for her, and they both stepped inside.

She excused herself to the washroom and was back quickly. Her skin glistened from her hurried arrival.

"I like the dress," Trent said. Her sundress looked cool and casual, and his compliment helped her settle into the evening.

"So how are you?" she asked as she patted his hands across the table.

"Good. You having a good week?" he asked.

"Well . . . it's been tough. Aunt Jo Anna is so depressed. The doctors have said she seems to be in remission. But she just lies in bed, even though nothing physical is keeping her from getting out and doing things. It's so hard on her children and all of us."

"When can I see her?" Trent asked.

"Whenever, I suppose. She isn't going anywhere."

"How late does she stay up?"

"All hours. She just watches TV and takes naps most of the day and night. It's so hard to watch. She has always been so full of energy and life."

"Want to do fast food on our way to Aunt Jo Anna's?" Trent asked.

She was already standing. "You're on." And they apologized to the hostess as the walked past her and out to Trent's car.

Kim called her aunt's home on their way over, and her cousin Jenna met them at the door. Jo Anna's room had screened double doors which looked over a pool, where lights played off palm trees, lawn furniture, and the rippled water. Kim cautiously stepped through the door in front of Trent.

"Hi, Aunt Jo Anna. How are you tonight?"

"Well, I'm here," she said wryly.

"Well, so am I, and I brought my new friend I told you about. His name is Trent, and he said he'd like to meet you."

"What is he, a masochist?" She offered a hollow laugh. "Welcome, Trent. Welcome to the pit of despair."

"Aunt Jo Anna loves *The Princess Bride*," Kim said, explaining the reference.

"As you wish," Trent returned.

"Oh, you've got a quick one here, Kimmy!"

"Yeah, I guess so," she said. "Hey, Aunt Jo Anna, I just thought you might like to meet Trent because he . . . well, he seems to know how to make people feel better."

"Can't be fixed, Trent. Sorry, I'm all broken like Humpty

Dumpty. Full of the junk." She turned to Kim. "He knows it's cancer, doesn't he?"

"Yeah, I heard that," said Trent, "and I'm no doctor or healer. I just like people. And I can already tell I like you."

"Oh, yeah, how's that?"

"You have a Giants pennant on the wall! I mean, anyone who lives in San Diego and is willing to advertise that they're a Giants fan has to be special," he said with a grin.

"You too?"

"Oh, yeah! Have been all my life."

"Me too," she said.

Trent was sensing a spark of hope. But then she grimaced as she repositioned herself in the bed. "Who are your favorite Giants ever?" he asked.

"When I was in school, I loved the Willies—you know, Mays and McCovey. And then there was Bobby Bonds." She paused and put her cupped hand to her mouth as if to tell him a secret. "And his boy Barry. I don't care what they say, I just loved him!"

Kim sat back in awe. The conversation was off and running between Trent and her despondent aunt. She left through the screen door and sat down by her startled cousin. Pointing her thumb toward Aunt Jo's room, she said, "Can you believe that? It's like they're old buddies."

Just then a burst of laughter came from the room. Jo Anna had sat up in bed and was slapping her knee. "No, no I'm not kidding!" she was saying. As they looked through the doors, they saw her stand from her bed and walk slowly toward the kitchen. "I tell you, I always have some."

"She's not going for the scotch, is she?" Jenna asked.

"Oh, Lord! I hope not. I haven't seen Trent drink anything," Kim said.

"Told you! Grab a couple of bowls out of the cupboard.

No, no, that one right there. Yeah, that's it," Jo Anna said.

The two cousins had stepped in and around the corner in time to see Jo Anna sit down at the kitchen table, setting down a frozen carton. "Here, you dip it, Frisco Kid!" Jo Anna snorted. "It's the real thing, cookies and cream!"

As Trent drove Kim back to her car, silence filled the cab. Nearing their exit, she said, "Thanks, Trent. I mean, you were wonderful. I thought things would be more serious and you'd be in her face like with that Carmen woman. But it was just perfect the way you cared for Aunt Jo. Perfect." She sat back again, reflecting on what she had just witnessed.

"Hey, Kim, remember I told you I'd be away this weekend? Well, I'd love another walk on the beach Thursday night if we could." Trent looked serious. "It's time I tell you more about my life."

"Hey, I know you like the Giants—yech! And cookies and cream ice cream. Then again, who doesn't? See, I know a lot about you, Trent," she said, smiling. Then she said more seriously, "I'd love to. And I may know something for sure by then from where I work. It's a surprise I want to tell you about."

"Start from my bungalow?"

"You're on." They were pulling up to her car. "She got out of bed and served ice cream! I just can't believe it!" She squeezed his thigh, shook her head, and stepped out of the car. "Ice cream!"

Trent hit the door of his home like he was on a high. He hadn't felt this way in a while. What was it? Was it Kim and the squeeze on the thigh? No. He knew better. This was about Jo Anna. This was about using his strengths. There was nothing as exhilarating to him as serving, showing love to people who needed love. And tonight he felt like he had raised the dead.

He sat by the pool and thought of the people back home who were facing their cancers, car accident recoveries, and other crises. Tonight he had given the best he had to give. But how many back home were hurting, feeling alone, while he was here in paradise? How was Natalie doing?

With that thought, he unlocked the door to his place and headed for bed. His mood had swung so hard his head spun.

Trent's days at work were often filled with intense labor, yet visible results. He enjoyed seeing the changes a day on the job made, productivity that increased now that he was managing three other employees. They seemed to enjoy meeting his early deadlines—and the benefits of extra time off and cash bonuses.

Tuesday and Thursday evening dates with Kim helped the remainder of the week before the retreat speed by. They had promised to go for another beach walk when he returned Sunday afternoon. Kim thought for sure she would know by then whatever it was she needed to know from work. Kim worked as a travel agent, and Trent had a few ideas about what she might be planning. Nothing he thought of seemed very appropriate. Maybe the weekend retreat would help him sort it all out.

Natalie remembered the retreats Trent often took for silence and reflection. He had a favorite spot in Wisconsin that welcomed clergy and their spouses. She decided to make reservations for her own weekend away. She would spend time praying for strength and direction. The fleeting thought of a Saturday evening rendezvous with Brandon slipped into her mind. But remembering her desire to get centered, she thought better of it. Of course, over the next few days, she couldn't help but spend some time imagining how such a rendezvous might go.

Everything about her times with Brandon felt exciting, enticing, and fun. Not much about these times felt right, however. Natalie wanted to straighten out her brain. But how could she be expected to think straight when her husband of fifteen years had just vanished into thin air? Surely God would forgive her any indiscretions. Still, she probably ought to get some wise counsel before leaping from the frying pan.

As Natalie drove north, she pulled into the drive-through of a fast food restaurant, and noticing that the line stretched around two thirds of the building, she decided to go inside. She had no deadlines, no reason to hurry. She was on retreat! A tall and tough-looking man held the door for her and stepped in behind her.

"Thank you," Natalie said.

"Welcome, ma'am. My pleasure," he said.

Balancing her food and drink on the plastic tray, Natalie chose a table where she could watch children playing on an indoor playground. The man sat across the aisle. "Beautiful day!" he said.

"Yes, it is," she replied.

"Well, I'm getting ready to head back home." He paused. "I'm from Georgia—Atlanta."

Bingo! Natalie thought. She had recognized the south in his accent. "That sounds good."

"Yep. Good and bad. It means I finished a job and have a check coming, but now I need to find another," he said. "I'm a private eye."

Natalie was thinking his pronunciation of "eye" sounded more the sound a patient makes when a doctor looks in his throat—"aah." She smiled at her thought, but decided it rude to express it out loud.

"I usually find deadbeat dads, you know, skipping out on their child support an' all," he chattered on around a mouthful of half-chewed french fries.

Natalie was thinking the fries looked good and the job sounded boring.

"Chased this feller's trail from Marietta, Georgia, all the way here to Janesville, Wisconsin. Should've seen his face when he knew he'd been had." He snickered and a partially chewed fry shot out onto his sandwich wrapper. He didn't seem to notice. "My name's Bender—Jake Bender."

Natalie almost didn't even notice him extending his hand. Her mind drew suddenly into focus around his occupation. "How much does it cost to find someone? I mean, like this guy you just found."

"Well, it's according to who's paying, ma'am. If it's the state, then sometimes it can be a good contract. With individuals, it's just according to what they can pay."

"My husband is missing. I think he's run off to California. And I need to find him," Natalie told him urgently.

"Tell me more," Jake Bender drawled as he swiveled his chair to face hers.

chapter 7

BLOODY BONES

T rent had looked forward to the weekend and his plans to go to a Roman Catholic retreat center. He was Protestant, but the Catholic Church always seemed to have places for getting away. He could go to this desert monastery and be left completely alone for forty-eight hours. He could practice solitude and silence.

After checking in, he collected his backpack and book bag and headed for his room on the second floor. A creaky old elevator stopped and its doors squawked open, but noticing the adjacent stairs, he opted for the exercise. After jogging up the stairs to his room, he shuffled open the sticky old door. The expectedly Spartan room smelled clean and was furnished by a single bed—with a crucifix hanging above—a rocking chair, a writing desk and chair, and a simple dresser. According to his habit, he began his retreat with thirty minutes of quiet sitting.

But Trent's mind raced even as he tried to settle it. He couldn't stop thinking about his old world—Natalie, the appointments he was missing this week, the people who would miss him. Then he thought of this new world: Kim, Nick and Allie, Nick's parents. Chuck—he needed to connect with him and thank him again soon. Darn! He hadn't even made it two minutes into his centering silence without his mind racing off, and he saw no peace in sight. He comforted himself with the reminder that retreats always started this way for him. Quieting himself was always tough, and would be tougher than usual tonight, considering his circumstances. But that was why he had come. *Two days from now,* he thought to himself, *I'll be centered and calm. Hang on.*

He had no idea how hard his stubborn spirit would resist the peace he sought.

Natalie arrived at her retreat center, moved her things into her room, and headed down to the lake. The motel-style center sat on a peninsula that stretched out into Lake Michigan. Chairs lined up along the beach, and a pier jutted into the waves. Kayaks and rowboats had been pulled haphazardly onto the shore, there for the taking. *If Trent were here, he'd be in a kayak,* she thought. Handling a boat alone in the rough waters was more than she felt she could do right now. It felt a little awkward here without Trent.

Stepping onto the pier, she walked out away from shore. The sky was clear and beautiful as far as her eyes could see. She looked up and down the coast; noticed fishing boats on the horizon, and heard a couple of Jet Skis approaching from her left. A teenage boy and girl were laughing and playing chase games on the expensive water toys. *Young love,* she mused.

She fingered the business card in her pocket and wondered if she should call the number. And with a sudden burst of determination, she removed her cell phone and confirmed that it had good signal. Then she sat down on the pier to make her call. She would do it. This guy must be good. After all, he had tracked someone from five states away.

Kim smiled as she jangled the bell on the front door of Harrod's Travel Company. She felt like skipping as she made her way to the space where she'd parked her Jetta. Hopping inside, she said aloud to herself, "He has to do this!"

Trent groaned and decided that in the history of measured time, no half-hour had ever lasted this long. Settling a mind, emptying it of endless details, was not a task for the faint of heart, and he felt more agitated than when he'd begun the quiet time. He was just admitting to himself what a grouch he must be right now when a gentle knock on his door shook him from his thoughts. "Yes?"

"I apologize for disturbing you, Mr. Atkins. Here are your towels. Sorry they weren't delivered before your arrival."

Trent opened the door and received the fresh-smelling delivery, and with a nod he thanked the monk who had brought them. Laying them on the dresser, he pulled out a pair of white socks and his walking shoes and put them on quickly, eager to escape the room. But as he placed his hand on the doorknob, a sudden lump in his throat nearly choked him. It was the socks. He remembered Natalie buying them. They had decided to begin walking together. Another false start in restoring their relationship, another disappointment.

He fell back into the rocking chair and decided not to fight the tears. Burying his face in the fresh towels, he began to weep. There were so many things he and Nat had planned. So many tender dreams they had never managed to bring to life. "Nat," he whispered into the silence, "you'd be happy to know I'm here. Trying to sort myself out. You would care to know that. I know you would. I . . . I. . . . " Then, pushing his face further into the comfort of the towels, he finished, "I never wanted to hurt you this way, Nattie. But we just can't be together. Can we?"

Jake Bender saw the message on his phone when he landed in Atlanta. He made the call as he rode the Metro toward home. Once inside, he threw his bag onto a chair, sat down with his laptop computer, and surfed his way through cheap, last-minute travel deals and sites specializing in snooping.

Early Saturday morning Jake was back at the airport. He called his mother with the news he'd be away another week, or however long it took. "Going to sunny San Diego," he told her.

Once aboard the plane, he squeezed into a window seat and prepared for a day with three takeoffs and landings on as many planes. He removed a file showing him Trent Atkins' final two weeks of debit card purchases before his mysterious disappearance. *Wonder if the chick Trent left for is as hot as the one he had?* he thought to himself.

He patted the file of answers Natalie had given him. He had data about everything from Trent's hobbies, favorite foods, automobile preferences, and a myriad of other details. *Here I come, Trent, my boy,* he mentally addressed his new target. *And I always get my man. Yep, just a matter of time. And son, from the looks of things, you won't be too tough.*

Trent knew it was too early in the retreat for clear thinking, but he wanted to begin a list. While considering possible futures that would utilize his gifts of caring, yet shelter him from the ravages of the pastorate, he thought of a few options. He wrote:

- *Teach Greek or some class on comparative religion in a university*
- *Keep my current job and join a house-church network*
- *Become a hospital chaplain*
- *Recognize myself for the failure that I am, give God a break, and get on with a regular life*

When he reread the last item in the list, he ripped the paper in two, wadded the pieces into the tiniest ball his strength could produce, and slammed it against the wall. Recognizing his agitation, Trent took a deep breath, let it out, and decided to take a walk on the grounds of the monastery.

Saint Joseph's was located well east of the city in the desert foothills. As he began walking from his lodgings, in only a few moments he was completely out of sight. Boulders and stones of varying size littered the grounds. Finding a suitable seat among them, he sat and began to think about how he would spend these days.

First, he had to get his mind to sit still and focus on his future. How would he enter this part of his life—what sort of foundations should he build on? What should remain of the old, and what would he need to build new? The overwhelming thoughts caused him to stand and walk again. He couldn't sit still, and his chest felt like it would explode with tension.

It wasn't unusual, he realized, to struggle at the beginning of his intentional retreats. Trent knew himself well enough to realize his restless spirit would resist centering, like a child fighting a much needed nap. *Lord, I'm so afraid to face myself and face your truth!* He wondered if Jesus ever struggled so mightily with prayer; and then he remembered Gethsemane.

Rounding a corner, he saw in the distance a striking formation of stone, with broad, flat rocks lying like dominoes at the end of a game. Drawing nearer, Trent could see what had been the foundation of an old church building. No sign of a roof or floor remained, only a course or two of stone marking the perimeter of the ancient chapel. He walked thoughtfully around it. Who had worshipped here? Who had built this? What priest had stood at the altar and led his congregants in worship?

The sound of footsteps in the sand jolted him from his

wonderings.

"Hello there. Sorry. Didn't mean to sneak up on you." An old priest had come upon him without Trent noticing.

"Oh, no, it's OK. I was just sort of getting the feel of the area here. Just got here for a weekend retreat, and I was looking around," Trent said. "I'm Trent. Trent Atkins."

"Father Timothy, Trent. Very good to meet you," the priest said in his thick Irish accent. It reminded Trent of his grandmother, who spoke in the same lilting brogue.

Trent took a step toward where the far wall of the chapel had once stood. Father Timothy spoke again. "Trent, if you don't mind my asking, what has brought you on this retreat? I would like to pray for you and help you as I'm able."

It was nice to speak to a stranger, especially such a kind one. Trent soon found himself unloading the story of his life in ministry—and his life with Natalie. He told of the new life he needed to build and expressed his firm resolve to build on the foundation of Christ. He had ruined his last start, he told Timothy, and felt ready to begin again. He told him of his gift of loving, of giving the grace of Christ to everyone he met, especially the unlovable.

Father Timothy listened quietly to what Trent had to say. Then he spoke softly. "It is good to come away to a place and pray about how you will build. It shows a wisdom that bodes well for your tomorrows. And I would believe all that you say about your purpose to build a 'selfless tomorrow' on an 'authentic today' if you were not so full of fear, my son."

"Fear?"

"Yes, fear. Trent, I'm afraid there is great fear in you. And one can't build well with fear in him."

"May I ask what you mean? Did I mention fear? I told you about my hopes and a firm resolve to do better—to do well with my tomorrows."

"Ah, yes, my boy. But that is the problem. Beyond this

ravine lies a beautiful monastery. Most of the stones from the old chapel that once stood where we are sitting were taken up there to rebuild something better." He paused, motioned up the mountain, and let out a deep sigh. His quaint accent nearly overwhelmed his speech. "Trent, my son, you have spoken about today and tomorrow. But you've not come clean about your yesterdays. I think you're afraid to. What stones do you not want to move into your new day, eh? What part of yesterday just can't make the trip into tomorrow? Because, my dear young brother, people aren't like buildings. If you tear away the building of a life from its foundation, you create pain in the new place as well as the old. Tell me, Trent, tell me about your yesterdays. What are you running from?"

Trent's head spun. The agitation returned, that feeling that something was biting at his heart. His first thoughts about this old priest had been tender; the wisdom he shared was so poignant. But now he felt angry and protective of his privacy. He turned on the old gentleman and said, "I came here to sort out my thinking about the future. I didn't ask for a spiritual director, or for a counselor. No offense, but I need this time for peace, not confrontation."

"Please," said the old priest, "don't make the bed of your future atop the bloody bones of your past, Trent."

Trent felt suddenly nauseated. Panic spread through his body. And his desire to run suddenly overtook his courtesy and better judgment. "I really need to get back to my room," he said. "Not feeling well. Sorry." And with that he jogged away from the man, wondering who he was and how he had climbed into his mind so quickly. "He had no right," he muttered to himself as he looked back over his shoulder, seeing nothing but aging stones and boulders that suddenly looked like fossilized old bones.

Jake Bender strolled slowly through the San Diego airport,

taking in all he saw. He studied the way people dressed, wore their hair, and walked. First item on tomorrow's agenda: new California-style wardrobe and haircut. Toting his bags along, he made his way outside to the line of waiting taxi cabs, boarded, and got lost into the flow of the city.

Natalie was almost too excited to sleep. She had come here to get away from her racing mind, but Jake Bender had given her hope of confronting Trent. As soon as he found him, Jake would call her immediately, and she would fly west and do the confronting herself. She didn't want him to have another chance to run. Not before she could speak her mind, show him how wrong he'd been.

As Natalie imagined the meeting, perhaps at his home or new workplace, she couldn't lay still in her bed. She considered walking to the pier and checking out the stars, or maybe going down to the lobby where there was a TV. She thought of going right to the airport and heading out to assist Jake's search efforts. She thought and twitched and turned until she could stay in bed no longer.

Did she just want to tell him off? Did she hope to catch him in some cheap romance? Did she want to let him know that she had a man who said he would love her forever? Did she want to tell him of the heartbreak at the church he had so summarily dumped into despair? All she knew was that she wanted to tell him. And tell him she would.

When Trent got back to his retreat room, he didn't know what to do. He was due at dinner, but feared that Father Timothy would be there. He hadn't planned to fast on this retreat, however, so he grabbed his wallet and keys and headed for the parking lot for a drive-through cheeseburger run. One paid meal wasted. The more he thought about it all, the more frustrated he got.

When he returned Trent went directly to his room,

packed his things back in his bag, and headed for the front desk. Cautious of his smart mouth, he grabbed a piece of paper and scribbled these words:

> *Dear Friends:*
> *I am afraid I'll be unable to stay with you this weekend. I had a rather difficult run-in with one of your priests—a Father Timothy—and I don't care to have another. Grace and peace to you all. Please keep my fees for another pilgrim to use.*
> *Reverend Trent Atkins*

He used his "Reverend" title in hopes of adding some sting to the communication. But he knew, even as he wrote the stabbing note, that he was being selfish. He felt the tension in his face and knew there was no grace or peace in his countenance. Nonetheless, he dropped his key at the desk and hopped back in his car. "I'm blowing Dodge," he murmured as he started the engine. He hadn't come here to have some stranger grill him about his past. Completely inappropriate! *Oh well,* he thought, *home on the beach is not such a hard place to go back to.* He couldn't have been more wrong.

On a whim, and since his plans had changed, he decided to call Kim. She wasn't home. Where was she? Why didn't she have her phone? And why did he care? He shook his head—he was acting like an addict. Heading west on I-8, he topped the mountain and dropped into El Cajon. He grabbed a large vanilla shake from a fast food joint—just what he needed. As he pulled out of the lot and back onto the road, rain crashed from the night sky. He could see lightning flashing in front of him as he headed toward San Diego.

By the time he pulled up to his bungalow, slashing wind had bent the palm trees nearly to the ground. After sitting for several minutes in his truck, he finally braved the run to the front door. Inside, he exasperatedly discovered he had left a window open. A whipping curtain had pulled a flower pot off the window ledge. It lay shattered on the floor in a puddle of mud.

Trent grabbed some beach towels to begin the cleanup and noticed a new message on his cell. His heart sank as he listened. "Hey, Trent. Since you're away, I decided to go with a friend to Rosarito, Mexico, for the weekend. Got free vouchers for the rooms and meals from work! I'll be back to my phone late Sunday night. See you next week, I hope. Oh, and Aunt Jo Anna is having a great day. She says you're the best man any woman has ever brought into her home. Hope you had a great weekend. I'll see you soon!"

Trent felt alone. His conscience condemned him into the night for leaving the hard work of the desert behind him only to find solitude waiting for him at home. Unsure of what else to do, he prayed the familiar prayer. He'd learned it on his first retreat and made it the center of his every prayer time: *Lord Jesus Christ, son of God, have mercy on me, a sinner.*

—To Tell the Truth

chapter 8

S aturday was fruitful for Jake Bender. By midmorning he had his new California look just right—his hair and wardrobe would blend in seamlessly, he was sure. Just before noon, he stopped by a branch of the state bureau of motor vehicles and met a young woman named Claire. She assured him no one could possibly hack into their secure files—and as she described their security systems in detail, she unwittingly filled him in on the tricks of cracking their codes.

By the end of the day, Jake knew that only one Trent Atkins had obtained a California drivers license in the San Diego area during the previous month. He'd also been able to pick up Trent's Social Security number and an address. As he drove past the address Trent had reported, Jake realized it was a work address, or a bogus one. At least he had a place to start on Monday morning. This job was going to be a cinch. Studying a picture of Trent, he said quietly, "You're going to be a piece of cake, bud."

He called Natalie's number and left her a message. "Hello, Mrs. Atkins. This is Jake Bender in California. I hope to have traveling news for you soon. Bye-bye."

By Saturday evening, Trent was ready for company. He set out to find a church service, and at 7:00 that night, he found himself on a kneeler at Saint David's by the Sea, praying silently, *Lord Jesus Christ, son of God, have mercy on me, a sinner.* The church offered communion for non-members, and Trent felt deeply grateful for the gift of the Eucharist.

Sunday he drove by Jo Anna's home, but lost the courage to stop in. He decided to go see Chuck and give him the long overdue thanks he had coming. He stopped on his way and bought him a pound of fresh roasted coffee. As he handed over the fragrant whole beans, Chuck commented about how much weight Trent had lost and how much sun he'd gotten. "You look like a California native, man!"

That evening, Kim called on her way back into town. Trent asked if she wanted to stop by, but she was tired and wanted to get home. They agreed to meet the next night for dinner at Trent's. She told him that the surprise she had mentioned was ready. She'd tell him at dinner. She couldn't wait.

Monday morning, Nick got a call from a Ken Ballard of the IRS in Memphis, trying to confirm that the company had hired a Trent Atkins in the past month. "We don't share our hiring information over the telephone," Nick said.

The southern gentleman advised Nick that he might want to think twice about not cooperating with the IRS, and it was then that Nick noticed his caller ID. "Hey, Mr. Ballard?"

"Yes, sir," answered Bender.

"Since when does the IRS in Memphis use a Georgia telephone number?"

The line went dead.

Jake Bender swore into the sky. How could he have been so stupid? He didn't make rookie mistakes!

Trent's cell phone rang. "Hey, dude, this is Nick."
"Yeah?" Trent answered.
"We need to meet for lunch. How about Old Town Café off of Hotel Circle at 11:30?"
"Sure, Nick. What's up?"
"Don't know, man. We'll talk."

Natalie's retreat finished better than it started. She found herself able to settle, knowing that she would soon catch up to Trent, and she relaxed and used a familiar prayer book, *Venite* by Robert Benson—given to her by Trent himself. Praying throughout the next two days—morning, noon, sundown, and bedtime—gave her some peace. But not far into her drive home from the retreat center, she noticed that a message from Jake had come through. Tension quickly overwhelmed her center.

She wasted no time getting a ticket from one of her travel agent friends at church. "With this, you can just go catch any flight that has an open seat, Natalie." Just what she wanted.

She called Jake Bender to tell him she'd secured a ticket. He sounded cross and reminded her not to call him. He'd call her if anything changed, but until then she needed to sit tight.

Trent felt a knot in his stomach as Nick told him of the mysterious call. They were both sure it wasn't the IRS, but Nick now had questions about his new dream employee. "What's up, Trent? Is there something I need to know about your past?"

Trent sat back. Then, tilting his head to make eye contact with Nick, he decided it was time. He had to tell Nick the whole story. He could no longer live only half honestly with his new friends. Trent told him who he really was, and by the end of the story, he felt miserable. He hated having admitted that his wife had been taken from him. He felt like a loser, and like a coward for having waited so long to come clean.

Nick seemed OK with the truth, but Trent could tell that his former occupation— the clergy—would change their relationship forever. It always did. He'd found that he just couldn't have real friendships with people outside of the faith once they found out he was a leader within it. He thought he noticed Nick pulling his shirtsleeve down to cover a tattoo Trent had seen a thousand times before.

They agreed to look for any suspicious people around the office or the job site, and to stay alert for any strange phone calls or anything that didn't seem to add up. The knot in Trent's stomach had become a boulder. *Bloody bones,* he could hear Father Timothy intone.

Jake spent the afternoon staking out the construction company address. No sign of anyone that looked anything like Trent's pictures.

"What's wrong, Trent?" Kim asked as they headed out to the beach. "You act like you don't feel well."

"Um . . . I guess I don't, Kim."

"I've never seen you like this. Is there something you need to talk about, or anything else I can do?"

"No. I'll be fine."

Still, he walked in silence and did not seem fine to Kim at all. Soon he realized that he was so preoccupied with the fake phone call at the office and what it might mean that he was sending cool, detached vibes to Kim. He wasn't being fair to her.

"Sorry, Kim. I-I just got some bad news today. Not really anything I want to talk about."

But Kim wasn't easily deterred. In fact, the strength she showed was just what Trent needed. "Physician, heal yourself," she said, a coy smile on her face. "You can pick others up out

82

of their crises, but you close yourself off when the going gets tough in your own life?"

"I'm sorry, Kim. I really feel lost, and believe me, you don't want to know what I'm up against."

"Oh, no. Believe me, I do want to know. Trent, in case you haven't noticed, I've become fond of you. Well, that sounded goofy. But truly, I enjoy our times together. I'm starting to think . . . well, that maybe we could have a future. Don't shell up and become all 'mystery man' with me now. Please. I don't need any more hurt."

Kim stepped in front of Trent, facing him. She placed her hands on his shoulders and leaned her forehead into his chest. "Tell me, please. What's happening, Trent?"

And so, for the second time that day, Trent unloaded his soul to a brand-new friend. This time, however, it wasn't merely an account of events, but a confession—a confession of his failures, desertion, and crash landing in San Diego. He had all of these ridiculous plans to build a new future on a disastrous foundation. He knew now that those plans wouldn't work. And it scared him.

She asked several questions about what had pushed him to his recent decisions. She asked about his career, what he had liked about it, what he had disliked about it, and why he was doing construction. She asked him how he felt about Natalie and, finally, how he felt about her.

"I wish I could run away one more time, Kim. I wish I could just start it all over with you on some crazy faraway island or something." He lifted her face toward his. "But if you went with me anywhere, you'd be running away with a quitter, someone you knew you could never really trust."

And then he turned away. She could tell he was beginning to cry. He dropped his beach chair and sat down in the sand. Quiet sobs shook his shoulders, and Kim could not stand by and watch. She sat beside him, and leaned into him, her arms around his shoulders.

"Here is what I know, Trent. First, I believe all of the words you have told me—all but the self-deprecating ones. Next, I don't believe there is any part of you that is mean or vicious or evil. I think you are a tender man, broken, but full of love. I also think you can't stand being anything less than perfect. You are the most caring and giving man I've ever met." She turned and looked into his eyes. "And I am determined to see you get your life back. If that means some girl named Natalie gets another crack at you, then so be it. But you need to know, I'm in this fight."

And then she pulled her face to his to kiss him, fighting through the wall of doubt in his eyes. But Trent looked away.

A long, awkward pause followed. And then the tension fell away with the tide and peace settled around them. She turned around to sit facing the same direction as Trent, and slowly he took her hand, savoring the electricity shooting through him. He felt torn, but just now, her hand in his anesthetized the pain.

He had to change the subject. "Hey, you mentioned a surprise or something."

"Well. . . ." She paused, wondering if the timing was completely wrong for her news. "I have a free trip for us. We can go on a cruise for as few as three days or up to two weeks. Of course, two weeks would be impossible with my schedule, and no doubt yours."

"As long as we're being honest, Kim, you need to know that my faith has kept me pretty sheltered. I am still a married man. I shouldn't be alone with you here, let alone out on a cruise ship." A few seconds of silence filled the space between them while he searched for the right words to say. "But I might want to hold on to that option for a while. Is that okay?"

"I understand, Trent. Let's take it slowly. Girls don't usually have that opportunity. Honestly, you have treated me
84

so kindly and with such . . . I don't know, I guess *honor* is the word. Well, that's why I'm falling for you. And now, you have a life to put together, and a past to make right. I'll stand by you, behind you, or, if I have to, on the other side of the country from you while you do what you have to do. I trust you."

Right or wrong, Trent held her in an embrace. It had been a long time since he had felt so fully known and yet so loved. "Kim, I can't tell you how good it feels to get this off my chest. I don't know where I'm headed, but I will always be grateful for the way you have cared for me tonight."

There were no words as they walked back, no holding of hands. They both seemed to understand they had crossed back over a line and needed to keep to their own sides. But there was no sense of a division between them. They were friends who had shared joys and laughter, conversations and comfortable silence, and now difficulties and darkness. And in that, they held a treasure they wouldn't forget.

Tuesday morning was a busy one at Nick's office. His receptionist peeked into his cubicle and told him about the visitor in the lobby.

Nick fired back, "Tell him to hold on. Give him some coffee or offer him a breakfast voucher for next door. I have to schedule another walk-through and get back on the Sampson project. It'll be another fifteen to thirty minutes." He didn't recognize the guy in the waiting area; in fact, something about the man was plain weird.

Thirty minutes later, Nick greeted Travis Johnson. "Sorry to keep you waiting, Mr. Johnson," he said. "How can we help you?"

"I'm looking for an old buddy of mine, and he told me he got a job here. Name's Trent Atkins. Your receptionist here told me I had the right place. Could you give me his number?

I don't want to bug him on a job site—unless that's not a problem."

Maybe it was the not-quite-right, peroxide-bleached hair, or maybe it was the thick Southern accent paired with a teenage-surfer outfit. In any case, Nick caught on quickly that he had spoken with this guy before. This was the IRS agent from Memphis, making calls from a Georgia number. "Tell you what, Mr. Ballard—"

"Johnson," Jake quickly corrected.

But Nick could see him start to sweat. "Tell you what, Mr. Johnson, Travis Johnson." Nick wrote on the back of a business flyer as he spoke. "I'll give him your number when he gets back in town. He's away for a while." Looking squarely at him, he added, "Your number?"

"Um, I'm using a friend's phone right now. I'd rather not give you the number. Could you just give me Trent's? He'd hate to miss me while I'm, um, down here in South California." As soon as he said it, he wanted the words back.

"Well, Trent isn't in *Southern* California right now. And something tells me he wouldn't mind missing you. I'm sorry, sir. I am very busy and I don't know what you are up to, but I just don't like it."

No sooner had Nick closed the door to his office than he called Trent. "Hey, buddy, this hick is out to get you. He was just here at the office. Just lie low. I'll get back with you later."

Jake decided to contact utility companies. He told them he worked for a marketing company and needed to know of new customers in the area. Obtaining a listing of all new connections during the past month in their San Diego market—at the price of a small fee for each item on the list—he racked up another serious chunk of change for Natalie.

Nick, Allie, Trent, and Kim had planned dinner that night at Nick's parent's poolside, a sort of reunion of the party just a couple of weeks ago that had introduced Trent and Kim. As the sky turned dark, Nick's parents went inside. Then Nick said urgently, "We need to talk, just the four of us."

They grabbed four chairs and walked out onto the beach. Arranging them in a circle, they leaned forward and awaited Nick's words.

"OK. Here it is. We all know your story, Trent. We believe in you and don't think this Ballard or Johnson guy is up to anything good. Maybe just a PI looking for you for your old boss or your ex. That doesn't matter. What does matter is getting you some time. Dude, you need to iron all this stuff out. If your wife is preparing a showdown, I'd like to see it on your terms, not hers."

Trent interrupted. "She probably deserves the advantage here, but I agree with you. I'd like to be able to back off for a week or so, then call her and set things up. I owe it to her, to myself, and all involved. I know I've screwed up. I just don't want to be accosted on what has been such friendly turf." He dropped his head. "I am so sorry for what you guys are dealing with."

"Trent, stop it," Kim said. "You know how much you've already meant to me. You've listened, you've turned my aunt's life back around, and I've even seen you do magic for a woman with an ugly ankle."

"Me too, dude! I'm just one more person who's really glad you're here. I'm grateful for what you've already done for the company. And Allie and I agree that you're great for my parents. They feel much more secure with you living here. You may even replace me in their affections." He grinned widely as Allie rolled her eyes. Kim leaned back and added, "Beware the classic Nick melodrama!"

"So here's how I see it," Nick continued. "Trent, we have to find a place to keep you where this guy can't find you. Ideas, anyone?"

"Uh, yeah. I have just the idea," said Kim. "Do you have a passport, Trent?"

"Yes. Why?"

"That cruise ship goes along the Mexican coast; it stops in Cabo San Lucas, Puerto Vallarta, and other nice spots. You can board anytime and stay on board for up to two weeks."

"If this guy is a hack, or a paid PI, he isn't going to like that wait, Trent," Nick said. "I think he'd go away if he knew you were gone that long."

"I can think of worse places to be in exile," Allie added.

"I could join you for part of the time, if you wouldn't mind, Trent," Kim said.

"Whoa, whoa. Hold on here. I mean, believe me, I'm grateful, but I don't know. . . ."

But an hour later it was all settled. Trent was outvoted, and the four made plans to stash him away for the next two weeks. Nick would see to his place and his few bills. All of them would watch for anyone suspicious. And in the meantime, they decided, Trent should work on that golfer tan of his.

Bender called Natalie's cell on Wednesday afternoon to give her the update he didn't want to give. "Hey, didn't want to have to leave this message, but I've run into a bit of a wall. Looks like I'm going to need some more time. Let me know if you want to call me off. The expenses here are on the high side. I'll send a first-week invoice on Saturday. Just need some direction. We'll get this done. Just may take another week or so."

Natalie didn't think he had the same confident tone he

had before.

Trent couldn't believe he was stowing his luggage in the cabin of a cruise ship. He wasn't sure what he would do with himself for the next few days, but he could sure think of worse problems to have. Still, even with the sun and fun that awaited him, part of him felt serious and sober. Before he came aboard, he'd taken a note to the post office.

> *Dear Natalie,*
>
> *Once again, I'm sorry for all I've put you through. I realize now just how selfish I've been. I plan to contact you within the next few weeks. It won't be this week. I'm sorry—it has to be this way. I care about the pain you're feeling and the trouble I've caused there. Don't know what else to say. Well, you won't find me. There seems to be someone trying . . . but you won't. I'm out of pocket right now. Believe it or not, I am praying for you. Peace.*
>
> *Trent*

Two days later, Natalie left a message for Jake Bender. "Get me the total costs so far, by this evening. I need receipts."

When he called with his current total, she told him she was buying out of the contract, per their agreement. She wanted him to drop the case. She trusted Trent when he said he would contact her. She no longer needed Jake's services.

Afterward, she called Brandon. "Hey, Bran, I have news."

chapter 9
————— OUT OF DODGE

J ust as Bender was dropping his pursuit of Trent and heading to the airport, Brandon was redoubling his efforts to win Natalie once and for all. He sent flowers with a note that read, "Praying for you and Trent." It killed him to write it, and he didn't mean it. He wasn't sure he was praying about Trent and Natalie at all; if so, he was praying for Trent to do something more stupid.

He called her the next evening and said, "I know the next week or two will be tough on you. Would you like to meet me in the city for dinner sometime? Anytime, Natalie, I mean it. I'm here for you, and you know I'm cheering for you."

She agreed, and they decided on dinner at her favorite pizza place, followed by a visiting Broadway show. He opened his laptop and went online to buy the tickets. *Perfect!*

Trent began a journal during his time away. He began to make lists. The first was headed *Things that made me run.* Under this heading, he began a list that spanned several topics and revealed more than he expected.

I've been angry at my work almost since I began. Why?

1. *When I became a pastor, I felt prepared to throw away my life for the sake of the gospel. I was all in. I was willing. I thought I was answering a calling; what I found instead was a career. And I felt like I was all alone. (I feel that I have more friends, and closer ones, here in San Diego after only a few weeks than I did at Baylor's Bend after eight years.)*

2. *Many pastors consider ministry just like any other job. Put in your forty hours—or, more realistically, seventy hours—and then go back to regular life the rest of the week. Grow the numbers of the church, be a good CEO, and raise money for better buildings. Move up to bigger churches at every opportunity you get. (This is called "God's will.")*

3. *Many people consider church a place to be entertained and educated and a place to make friends. The idea of giving themselves to others outside of the church doesn't appeal to them. Buy new playground equipment for their kids, hire staff to counsel and console their teens, and call on their nursing home residents once a month or so, and they'll be happy. If you don't please them, they'll move to another church. (This is called church-hopping.)*

4. *After years of trying to impress and please everyone with my hard work, I was tired.*

5. *I found myself turning bitter. All of the above made me want to scream, but I couldn't complain about my job to anyone. Not Natalie. Not anyone in the church. Not my staff. Not my bishop. How would I appear to them if I showed frustration or weakness? I was so alone. Even my lonely times since leaving have not felt so difficult as those long stretches of loneliness I felt as a pastor.*

6. *I had to always be "up" and positive. The constant and subtle lie that I wasn't allowed to show weakness or struggle burned holes in me.*

7. *Even Natalie didn't want to hear about the hard times and seemed to expect superhuman strength from me. Maybe because she had her own agenda. She was in love with being the queen bee of the church and wouldn't hear of me quitting or finding another way to do ministry besides being a pastor. I couldn't even speak of being on the support staff, instead of senior pastor, at another church. She needed me to be the big guy. (She often spoke of Brandon needing to finish his degree so he could be a "real" pastor!)*

8. *I felt trapped. I would often dream of doing something different with my life, anything to earn a living. (When Nat didn't listen, I would just quietly dream of these options until finally I plotted my childish escape. Hmm— "childish." Maybe I have been a little immature—I can admit that. But I refuse to forget how desperate I was—how desperate I am. I'll never crawl back into the same crack again. It is too hard to get out.)*

9. *I have never faced my inability to confront. I am weak. When conflict would arise in the church, I just **could not** face people with strength. I should have gotten help, counseling, or whatever. Instead, I buried my anger or my opinions. When people confronted me, I couldn't stand up for myself. Instead I'd take the supposedly humble way out and say that they were right. Saying, "I'm sorry" was easier than saying, "Hey, why don't we look at it from my standpoint?" And people confronted me all the time with all kinds of things. A few examples of expectations I tried to live up to:*

- *Some people thought I needed to be out of bed and active by 5:00 AM. They would call to check occasionally. Others thought they should be able to call me until 11:30 PM. "Everyone stays up until after the news," they said. Just because I'm awake doesn't mean I'm at work.*

- *People had opinions on whether or not I should wear shorts or sandals, or whether I should go to movies or dance with my wife at public events, or whether I should wear a ring besides my wedding ring.*

- *Some people thought I should be in the office from eight to five daily. "What if we need to stop by to see you?" (And that they did. When I was at the office, friendly visits were nice, but if I needed to leave or get back to studying, they felt brushed off, like I didn't care.) Others said I should be out in the community, reaching out. Still others thought I should keep up with the exacting schedules that the former pastor kept.*

- *One committee told me that I made too big of a deal about spending time with Natalie. They thought I shouldn't tell people that Friday night (my day off) was our date night. So I caved and began to visit parties and get together with other couples on my day off. The same committee told me they worked sixty-plus hours at their jobs, then added fifteen per week at the church. They said I should be putting in at least as much time as them, which amounted to seventy-five hours—besides service times—each week. So I did. They didn't know that during all those hours that didn't count in my total, I had my mind on the hurts of the people, the fears and gossip they relayed to me.*

I was a weakling. The only way I could get tough was to bottle stuff up and then let the cork blow. (Not with confrontation, of course. I decided to run instead.)

Bloody bones. I haven't been able to forget that analogy since Father Timothy used it. I can't just run from the past. He didn't mean that I had to pack the bones back into my same old life; he meant I need to deal with them before I start over. But instead of hearing him, what did I do? I ran!

So here are some things I need to resolve:

- *I must make things right with Natalie— communicate our way back into or out of our relationship. I simply must have some kind of say. She wouldn't see a counselor, but I'm guessing her pride is bruised enough that outside help won't seem so intimidating now. I want to hear her side, but I have to share mine as well. (It seems that making things right between us has always required me to give in. I'll give where I need to. But I won't subject my soul to any role that doesn't jibe with what seems to be truth about me, about us. I will be actively involved in thinking about my future. I won't just accept whatever she says.)*
- *I must be honest about my call to ministry. I must obey God. And I no longer believe that means I have to be a CEO in the church business or a Sunday morning entertainer and program director. (Hymns or choruses? I am*

finished throwing my passions into people who think this issue is larger than the needs of those around them.) Never mind the constant pressure to raise money to pay for buildings we use once or twice per week. A mortgage payment of over $10,000 per month for seventy-five families to have the facility they think they need? (And then I had to cajole them into meeting our giving goals in order to raise enough to pay the mortgage payments.) Honestly, from where I sit right now, I don't know if I'll ever get this figured out.

- *My own consistent problem with confrontation. I am unable to look someone in the eyes and express disagreement with that person. I want them to love me (like me), so I let them think I agree with everything they do or say. Even when they condemn me, I can't stand up for what I know is right. (Not that I'm always right, but during my fifteen years there, I think I was probably in the right a time or two!)*

- *Running. Since I hate to disappoint people and can't confront them, I chose to run. I can't do this again. Not in this ridiculous earthquake way, and not in the thousands of tiny ways I must do it every day.*

Natalie has paid a horrible price. How did we begin to drift apart in the first place?

1. *We didn't disagree well. I wouldn't tell her my disappointments, and when she tried to tell me hers, I took any complaint as a personal assault. I could not communicate. Couldn't speak in truth. Didn't let her. (Ouch! Is all that true?)*

2. *So she learned to not expect truth from me, and to communicate to me by manipulation. She graduated from pouting, angry silence, and coldness to rejecting me in bed.*

3. *When I did mention my frustrations with our relationship and wanted counseling, she didn't want to admit we needed it. Thought it would look bad for the pastor to go to counseling. "What if they find out?" she said. (Of course I didn't stand up for myself and insist.)*

4. *When I did mention my frustrations with ministry, she would try and talk me into staying with it. "You are soooo good at it. You love these people. What else could you do?" Which meant: "With your seven years of education toward this job, you have no other way to earn a living! What would we do for money?" At first this threat was all I needed. I knew we couldn't get by without my income. But the longer I thought about it all, the less I cared if I was poor. Living very simply began to sound better than living with all these material comforts, but otherwise not living.*

(Is that last phrase overstated? Was I not really living when I lived back home? As I look back, I don't think I was. I dreaded every day—especially Sundays. I could barely even think about anything that wasn't work related, until I adopted my hobby horse of planning an escape. For now, I stand behind the phrase "not living" to describe my former life.)

Trent felt exhausted after writing out all this introspection. Yet after recording his thoughts, he felt better—maybe not cleansed, exactly, but better. Clearer. Realizing that he was about ten steps away from a breathtaking view of the ocean, he decided to take a break from journaling, throw on his

Birkenstocks, and go explore the ship.

Kim had wondered what Trent thought of her joining him aboard at the end of the first week. He seemed happy, but quiet, a little unsure. Her boss encouraged her to go and made sure they would have separate quarters, much to Trent's relief. *Christians are so funny about that stuff. It's not like I'd expect to sleep with him,* Kim thought.

She sincerely hoped he could find peace with Natalie. In truth, she hoped only for peace, not a full reconciliation, but she didn't want to steal from Trent a resolve that she had never known in her own marriage. It seemed right to keep him cared for, but free. She knew one thing for sure: she looked forward to the time away with him.

Natalie had lots of time to think. Her night on the town with Brandon was wonderful. She couldn't help but tell her mother about the Broadway show, although she told her she had met an old friend in the city. (Emma didn't think to ask further.) But as much as she enjoyed the play and a nice dinner, Brandon was the highlight of the evening. She felt he understood her. They communicated better than she ever had with Trent. And Trent would never take the time to go to a play. Even if he did, he would talk about work on the trip there and back.

In fact, the more she thought about their marriage, the more she realized that their entire life had centered on his work. She could hear him drone on as they traveled to their latest conference. "Do you think we could try clowns during next year's Bible school? Do you think we could grow the Sunday school if we did a class about raising pre-schoolers? Do you think the music was good enough this week? What were we thinking hiring Kent as a children's worker? He doesn't know how to put in a day's work." And on and on he would go.

Brandon, on the other hand, cared about her. He would

ask about her work and tell her how much he loved her singing, and he actually spent the entire drive home talking about the plot development of the play they'd seen, rather than asking if they should paint the church nursery again. Trent might have left, and she would certainly like to give him a mouthful, but things were turning out just fine.

She decided to send Brandon a card. "Thanks for the good time," read the message on the inside. On the opposite panel, she wrote:

> *I can't tell you how much I enjoyed our evening in Chicago. You are such a good listener, and you sure know how to pick a restaurant! The play was wonderful, and the discussion on the way home was awesome. You should write reviews for the Tribune!*
> *Natalie*

She was feeling better already.

Trent had never felt such intense sun. He pulled the collar of his polo shirt up around his neck as if that would offer the protection he needed. He stopped by the on-board pharmacy for sunblock.

Nearing the bow of the ship, he found several empty chairs and pulled a lounger to the spot he wanted. From here he could see, but barely hear children playing in a pool to his left, or he could gaze into the vast distance of the Pacific before him. Relaxing into the umbrella-covered chaise, his eyes grew heavy and he fell into a gentle sleep.

Twenty minutes later, he awoke to loud laughter. A group of men had gathered around a table beside him. He tried just lying there and feigning sleep. But the men kept talking and laughing and only grew louder, and soon he could no longer pretend they weren't there. He stirred and got up to leave.

"Hope we didn't wake you," one of them said.

"No, no. Well, yeah, but I really needed to get going," he said, glancing at his watch. *Even here,* he thought, *I have to make a pretense about busy-ness. It's like I'm conditioned to do it after years of church work.* It reminded him of another set of entries he needed make in his journal.

"You look like you could fit right in this circle," the same speaker, a larger gentleman, mused, obviously discerning that Trent had a few things in common with the men at the table. From head to toe, the man looked like the stereotypical pastor. "Mind if I ask what you do for a living?"

Suddenly it was important to Trent to appear professional. He decided to stretch the truth and play his hunch about who these men were. "Well, actually, I'm on a sort of a surprise sabbatical," he said. "But my job, um . . . I'm a pastor."

"No kidding," said a younger guy who looked like a youth worker. "That's what we all thought!"

The first guy spoke up again. "Yeah, my staff and I decided to get away for awhile, and our church said they'd put us out here on this big, beautiful thing," his deep voice boasted, as he dramatically held his hands out across the deck of the ship and grinned. Trent felt it coming. "Isn't God good?" the pastor enthused. Yep, there it was. The gentleman stuck out his hand to shake Trent's.

"Um, yeah," Trent said flatly. "So where are you guys from?"

"The Phoenix area," youth guy said. "You?"

"Oh, So Cal," he said, trying to sound cool.

"Cool. We boarded this baby in San Diego. Love it! Of course I guess we 'zonies' are known for that, huh?" "Zonies"— the not-so-loving term Southern California people use to refer to the hordes who escape the Arizona desert, further crowding California beaches and coastal towns.

Trent had never heard the term. "Um, yeah."

"So what church are you with?" the senior pastor asked.

Trent knew where this would go. The next question would seek to know the size of his congregation. After that was established, they'd ask about what kind of church he served, and these guys would probably know someone in his denomination from San Diego—someone whom, if he were a real and active pastor here, he should know. Trent pointed to the sweeping horizon and said, "I'm out here trying to forget all of that, gentlemen. Don't ask me about work, and I'll return the favor." He smiled a big pastor smile.

They went for it. "Yeah, we need to learn that skill, man. We've been out here looking at statistics and working on our staff dress code. You know, trying to find another way to run a tighter ship." A new guy speaking. Music minister?

Trent took the opportunity to make his escape. "Hey, guys, got to get going. Hope to see you around." And with that he headed toward the stairs and the gift shop. *Whew!* he thought. *Any longer and I would have had to tell them how many members I "have," how much cash we raise each year, and how large my campus is. This is exactly what I'm running from! Always the ABC's: Attendance, Buildings, and Cash.*

Brandon had known Natalie for several years. And he had wanted her since they met. Trent hired Brandon to run the music program shortly after taking on the role of senior pastor. From the very first, Natalie worked on Brandon's music team, and they hit it off. He had kept his thoughts to himself, knowing it was just a silly fantasy. But in recent years, as her marriage had struggled, Brandon was the one she had chosen to talk to.

He had waited patiently for too long. Now the prize of her affections was his. But danger still lurked. When Natalie told him about the call she expected from Trent within the next couple of weeks, he nearly panicked. He couldn't come this far and lose Natalie. She had reassured him, repeatedly insisting that she was "over" Trent. But she could be a funny girl, and he feared the prospect of her flip-flopping and falling for Trent once again.

The idea had occurred to him soon after Trent's departure. He had dismissed it as ridiculous. But the closer the time came to Natalie speaking with Trent again, the more his idea appealed to him. Maybe it wasn't so ridiculous after all.

He kept back editions of the *Chicago Tribune* for recycling. His stack was now well over a month old, and he knew he had the issue for the week Trent had skipped town. Thumbing to the local crime section, he began to read. There were no shortages of bad things happening in a city the size of Chicago. But whatever he chose had to be believable.

About halfway down the front page of the section, the bold headline read, "Patient Found Dead." He read on.

Nurses at St. John's Medical Center were shocked to find a patient (name withheld) dead when they entered her room yesterday afternoon. Hospital spokesperson Renee Simpson said the patient was preparing to go home that afternoon after having outpatient surgery earlier in the day. The victim's pillow was found on the floor next to her bed and an intentional smothering seems possible, Detective Jimmy Strand of the Chicago Police Department told the Tribune. *On condition of anonymity, a staff member from the hospital told the* Tribune *that the victim was an employee of the federal government.*

Quickly Brandon ran back out into his garage to check the next day's paper. He leaned intently over the paper when he saw the headline. "Patient Death Ruled Murder."

Chicago police Detective Jimmy Strand said in a news briefing today that the death of an Oak Grove woman at Saint John's Med Center is believed to be a murder. The woman appeared to have been sexually molested and then smothered to death. The department is looking for clues in the murder, but so far has no leads.

This was certainly a stretch, but Brandon needed something big—something that would do serious damage to Trent's reputation. Sitting on the bottom step in his garage with the newspaper lying on his knees, he pursed his lips, folded the paper, and set it aside.

Brandon hopped in his car and headed for the church offices, accelerating fiercely through the city streets. Everyone was gone for the day. He ran along the hallway leading back around the sanctuary to the offices. Looking around again to make sure no one was watching, he stepped to Miss Simpson's desk. Grabbing the calendar she kept, he threw it open to the page showing the day Trent left. Where was his schedule? Here it was. First item: "9:00 AM—Ellen Jenkins, 9:45 surgery."

"What hospital?" Brandon shouted aloud to the room. "Jenkins, Jenkins . . . " he murmured as he rifled through the church directory pages. He punched in the number desperately, swiveled around in the secretary's chair, and waited for the answer.

"Hello?"

He covered the receiver and cleared his throat. "Hello. Jess?"

"Yep. This Brandon? Saw the number on caller ID."

Darn. "Yes. How are you doing, Jess?"

"Oh, OK, I guess, considering everything."

"Yeah. Well, hey, I was just wanting to call and check up on you guys, on Ellen and all. I mean, she had surgery the day Pastor Atkins left. Just wanted to make sure you two were OK."

"Sure. He came to see her, you know. He was a little late, but so was the surgery. Was just his normal self, you know—very kind and attentive. I was there, of course. He just came in, and it seemed like everything was OK after that. We knew he was busy. But he just always seemed to have the time to look you in the eyes and see how you were doing. Well, he cared for us, prayed for Ellen, and sat with me and the girls until the surgery was done. And then he waited until Ellen was out of recovery. Then, just the way Pastor Trent always does—well *did*, I guess—he prayed with us, and then he was on his way. Oh, we sure do miss him!"

"Oh, we all do! The staff is just lost without him," Brandon blurted. "Hey, I just wanted to make sure she's recovered well and all."

"Oh, yes. She's fine."

"What did you think of the service you got from the hospital?" *Did that sound lame? Why would I ask that?* Brandon thought.

"Oh, we've always liked the care we get there. Yep, it's been years ago, but both of our kids were born at Saint John's."

"Well, great. Absolutely great, Jess. I'm glad she's doing well, and I suppose I'd better let you go now." He placed the receiver back in its cradle and did a fist pump. "Bingo! It was Saint John's!" he said aloud.

That evening at dinner, Trent chose an Italian buffet. He felt a bit awkward sitting alone, especially when the church staff retreat pulled up to a table next to his. "Yer wife here?" the stereotypical senior pastor asked.

"No. Doing some alone time."

"Well, then, join us! Sorry, I forgot to introduce myself.

I'm Brother Jim Johnson."

"Uh, Trent . . . Trent Atkins is my name." And he reluctantly slid over to a chair around their dinner table.

"Youth guy," as Trent had dubbed him, was really "Brother Chad." "Music guy" (Trent had nailed it) was Roger. And the children's minister was Reggie.

The evening began enjoyably, to Trent's surprise. The meal was delicious, and the table partners managed to keep the chat light, although they seemed to find it impossible to complete two sentences without going into church matters. Trent remembered it all too well. *When you're in this business,* he thought, *you have no other life.*

Shortly before he worked up the courage to make his exit, they began asking more about Trent. It seemed the more he tried to keep distant, the more he felt the pull of truth. He had no experience lying or hiding things. Not until recently, anyway. And as the evening wore on, his resistance wore thin, and he considered sharing the truth about who he was and what he was doing on this cruise ship.

As he weighed the pros and cons of self-revelation, a man stumbled into their table. "Thsorrrry for the bump!" he snickered. He was stone drunk. "My wifthes a-a-angry wifth me."

At that a beautiful woman came to his side. "Phil, come on. You are drunk!" The urgency in her voice was in a crescendo matched by her volume.

"Aw, Maggie. I ain't drunk. Am I, fellas? Juthst makin' some new friends."

Reverend Jim Johnson stood. "You're at the wrong table. Get away now." He shooed him with a flick of his wrist. "You're drunk." His staff sat dumbly, looking back and forth between their leader and the drunk man.

Trent stood. "No need for that, Jim. Hold on." He turned to the woman. "I'll see if I can help."

The woman began to sob. "Please do come with me, honey. Let's go back to our room."

Then Trent said to the drunk man, "Friend, I was just planning to walk back to my room. Come on, old buddy, join me!" He picked up his glass of soda and made a toasting motion, as if promising another round at the bar.

The man said, "OK, buddy." Looking to his wife, he pointed to Trent and said "*This* is my good friend!" And turning to the table of men, he said, "Cheers!" while lifting an imaginary glass, then throwing an arm around Trent's neck.

"Thank you," Maggie whispered.

When Trent had finally deposited the man through his doorway, he sighed and headed toward his own.

The homicide detective had the habit of bringing his work home with him. After the late-night news, he grabbed a file he'd brought home from the office. Inside was a small envelope with his name on the outside. The desk clerk had said someone dropped it off earlier that day. Tearing it open, he looked at the printed message.

> *FYI. Reverend Trent Atkins was at Saint John's hospital on the morning of the murder I've read about in the paper. Later that day he disappeared from his wife and congregation. He is believed to be somewhere in Southern California.*

As the ship prepared to sail from Cabo San Lucas, the final leg of the journey for most cruisers had begun. Trent had found another lounge chair to watch passengers re-boarding. He was embarrassed when he realized he had stared so intently at a dark-haired beauty on the far side of the deck as she passed by. He didn't think of himself as a girl watcher. As the woman walked around the corner, he had to grin at himself—nearly every man in sight had turned his head as she walked past. The woman in the turquoise sundress had cast her spell on all of them.

Soon the captain announced the departure, and Trent headed back to his room to prepare for dinner. Arriving at his door, he found a *Do Not Disturb* sign. He double checked to see if he had the right cabin. He did. As he turned the key and opened the door, he stood eye to eye with the girl in the turquoise sundress.

"*¡Buenos tardes, amigo!*" Kim greeted him with a festive grin. "*¿Cómo estás?*"

"Kim! What, um . . . what are you doing here?"

"Surprising you. I was able to jump on board a few days early, so thought I would! Hope it's OK," she said. "Just couldn't stand the thought of you being exiled out here all alone." She put a cute, pouting look on her face.

"Well, it is good to see you, I just . . . " Trent was looking around the room, and at her luggage.

"Not to worry, Trent. We have a different room. Let's go see it. I couldn't get separate quarters, but I did get the 'High Seas Suite'! We'll have separate rooms, a sitting area, and the whole deal. This is high roller territory!"

Trent didn't know what to say. He knew she was giving him a wonderful gift with the cruise, and he knew the separate-rooms issue had been addressed, even though they would be staying only a few feet apart. But something continued to pester him. He couldn't figure out if he was hung up on how it looked for them to be together—as if he knew anyone on the ship, or as if anyone cared—or if he was struggling with trusting himself with the belle of the cruise.

"Well, let's go see it!" Kim said. "We can come get your things in a minute."

They grabbed her bags and were off. The suite was not

large, but it did have two separate, if tiny, sleeping areas for them. She was excited, and he started to relax with the idea.

"I guess I'll run back and pack my stuff." He didn't know if this was real or not. It reminded him of a teenage fantasy.

"OK. Oh, and here's a piece of mail that came after you left."

He took the envelope and started toward his room. Shielding his eyes from the bright evening sun, he tried to read the return address. As Trent walked under an eave, the script became clearer. It was a letter from Saint Joseph's. Trent rolled his eyes and realized that his overreaction was now receiving a reaction of its own. He almost didn't want to open it, but he did.

Dear Reverend Atkins:

Please accept our apologies for your brief and, as it sounds, unpleasant visit. At Saint Joseph's we pride ourselves in providing exquisite service to every pilgrim who comes our way. We wish to treat them as we would treat Christ. Your unfortunate run-in is both disappointing and confusing to us. You see, we have no Father Timothy here, and there were none visiting us at the time. In fact, the last Father Timothy we have record of here is the founding priest who started our monastery from an old chapel where he served. It sits out in the desert a short walk from our current campus. Perhaps there was a visiting priest passing through that day.

If you are able to come again soon, we would welcome you with open arms, yet give you all of the distance you need to wonder, sit, pray, and wander.

Once again, please accept our apologies and the invitation to try retreating here again soon.
Grace and peace to you,
The Staff at Saint Joseph's

Trent folded the letter and placed it back in the envelope with a shiver, one that continued to run along his back and arms for a moment or so. Who was Father Timothy? He knew only one thing for sure: the man he had met that day by the old chapel had given him the kindest and most poignant message he could have received. Father Timothy, whoever he was, had spoken truth to him.

As Trent arrived back at the suite, Kim was putting the last of her things away in the rear quarters. "You look like you've seen a ghost!" she said.

"Yeah. Well, maybe I have," he said, almost to himself. "This my place?" he asked, pointing at the front room.

"That's it. Isn't it great?"

"Absolutely. Great, yeah, it's beautiful."

"I'm not convinced. What's up, Trent?"

"Nothing really. I'm just a little overwhelmed. It's a good overwhelmed. I mean, I have someone to talk to now, and the letter was kind of nice to get. I guess I'm just surprised." He thought he was making a nice recovery. He felt startled by the letter—and by Kim—but he didn't know how to explain it, and he didn't want to cast a shadow on her surprise. "Thanks for coming. Thanks for this incredible trip and for everything, Kim. I don't mean to be ungrateful. My life is just kind of . . . well, I don't know what it is."

"Aw, I should be more understanding. Of course you're overwhelmed. Listen, don't mind me. This trip is for you. I'm here for you, and if I need to be close, distant, or whatever, just let me know," she said. And then she stepped forward, took his bag from him, and threw it on his bed, then hugged him. "You are an incredible man, and I am your friend, no matter what."

After tucking his things into the new room, they walked back out into the bright sunlight. Just as they exited the room, something happened that Trent could not have predicted.

"You must be Sister Atkins!"

It was Jim Johnson, senior pastor, holding out his hand to shake Kim's. All she could do was turn and look at Trent. And all Trent could do was look horrified.

Natalie waited for Brandon on a park bench near the art museum. She had taken the train in from Matteson, and he was driving to meet her. They had plans to spend the afternoon at the museum and then have dinner on Michigan Avenue. As she waited, she listened to a group of boys giving a virtuoso performance drumming on five-gallon plastic buckets. Crowds came and went as the boys played for tips.

She had become thoroughly engrossed when she felt a hand on her shoulder. "Hey you!" Brandon said. "Pretty tight rhythms, huh?"

"Yes. It's hypnotic! I've listened for a half hour now, and they haven't repeated a thing."

As they walked, Brandon's hand bumped Natalie's, and she recognized the invitation. She decided to wait until they were sitting safely in a restaurant booth, out of the view of any unlikely acquaintance. Then she would take his hand in a heartbeat. And she would tell him what the lawyer had told her today. The divorce was moving along as quickly as possible. It wouldn't be long.

chapter 10

DARK NIGHT

After Trent told Kim that the stranger had called her "Sister" because he'd told him he was a pastor, she squealed with laughter. When she realized the guy thought she was the reverend's spouse and not his sibling, she laughed even harder. Trent soon had to laugh at the situation himself.

But as the evening wore on, he grew more withdrawn. Kim labored under his mood, trying to cheer him with jokes about their "marriage." Realizing that it didn't help, she asked him why he was so down.

"I'm just lost, Kim. Here I am with you on a cruise, of all things, wishing this were my real life. I'm wishing that in some alternative life, you and I would have met and would be together . . . you know, married. I'm living in a fantasyland, Kim. None of this is real." He looked like he could either cry or walk away at any moment.

"Let's take a walk, Trent. You look like you could use a promenade along the deck of a beautiful ocean liner at sundown. And I can offer you that right now, even if I can't offer you anything else." She stood and smiled in a way that indicated she intended to have her way on this.

"Yeah, OK," he relented.

They stepped to a rail near the portside bow. They stood and stared as the sun began to slip behind the green sea on the horizon.

Trent spoke softly. "I can't live artificial stuff. That's what drove me here. My work became a fake thing. My marriage had become pretend. My smiles were forced. And my heart became absolutely selfish. So selfish I hopped on a plane without offering any explanation to those I loved, and I disappeared."

Things were quiet for a moment. Kim wanted so badly to put a hand on his shoulder, but was half afraid it might fragment and half afraid she would be misunderstood. So she stood and waited, pressing the side of her arm tighter into his as they both leaned into the rail.

He began again. "I feel like I acted just like a kid on the playground. When things aren't going his way, he just takes his ball and goes home. 'Fine! No one can play, then.' How childish is that?"

She let the words fade for a moment, then thought of a response. "Perhaps it's like a child who was being abused by bullies on the playground and left for a safe place." Silence. Then, "Trent, you are not artificial. You are authentic. The things I've seen in you are not fake. You could have just come here and conned us. You could have made up a lie about your past and moved on into the new family that surrounds you here. But you didn't. You are too real for that. You, Trent. You are not artificial."

She decided to stay with this. It was making sense to her. "Really, now, listen to me. I've seen the way you give, the way you serve, and the way that you love. Complete strangers find themselves embraced in loving care when you're nearby. If there ever was anyone who should be a God-guy," she stopped, realizing that was not a real title. Starting over, she said, "If there ever was anyone who should be a pastor—although to me, that title just doesn't sound right for you—it would be you. You represent God so well. You are a good 'God-guy.'" She grinned, enjoying the new term she had coined.

"I've got to get on with this, Kim. I mean, the whole process of working all this out. I have to call Natalie, arrange a meeting, and begin to settle all of this. I should make the call tonight! Any reason you can think of to wait? I mean, my conscience is killing me."

"Can't think of any, I guess. You did come out here to get away and think, but if this is clouding your thinking, it seems to me you might as well get on with it."

"I think I will." And he turned away and walked back toward his room.

Brandon was furious. Every since she received Trent's note saying he would call soon, she had seemed distant. When Brandon called her on it, Natalie would say she was thinking about what to say to Trent; she just wanted to tell him off, let him have it. But any communication between Trent and Natalie presented too high a risk—too high for Brandon's comfort, anyway.

He wanted Natalie free to pursue a new future, the future he was pursuing. He could think of nothing else. Every day he was disappointed when he turned to the crime page of the newspaper. Nothing more about that homicide at Saint John's, nothing! Had they solved the case?

And then, three days after Natalie received Trent's note through Dr. Phillips, he saw it.

Hospital Murder Lead. *Chicago Police Detective Strand said today that the department is cooperating with the FBI in regard to a lead in last month's murder of a Saint John's patient. An anonymous tip led to a potential suspect who is wanted for questioning. Police have been in touch with a private investigator from Georgia who is believed to have worked on a related missing persons case.*

Trent's heart was about to beat through his chest as he dialed the number. Would she be there? Would she answer? Had she moved out? He steadied himself by grasping the headboard as he heard the so familiar message play for his telephone. It was Natalie's voice. "We're not in right now. Please leave a message, and we will be happy to get back with you as soon as we can." He braced himself to leave his reply.

"Nat, it's me. I was hoping we could talk. I will try your cell phone."

Well, that did it. She could use her caller ID to find his new number. He was no longer on the loose. Probably the phone company could even track his call to this location. What would she think if she heard he was on a cruise ship? He knew what she'd think: that he'd never been willing to take her on a cruise.

Before he lost the courage, he dialed her cell number. On the second ring, he heard the click of the call being received, and then "Hello?" It was her voice. For the first time in a decade, it froze him.

"He-hello, Natalie?"

"Who is this?" she demanded. But he could tell by her voice that she was shocked, relieved, and angry all at the same time. She knew who it was.

"Nat, it's me, Trent. I'm . . . I'm sorry for this stupid situation." He swallowed.

"Trent. You have no idea what . . . " Her voice went away, and he could hear her sobbing. And then through the tears, she managed, "Where are you?"

"I'm out west, Nat."

"I know that! I mean, I know that's where you've been.

When are you coming back?"

Coming back. The words sounded somehow ominous to Trent. "Well, Nat, I'm wanting to plan that now. How do you want to meet? Do you want me to just meet you near the airport? Do you want to meet alone or with someone else—like Dr. Phillips or something? I'm not sure how to handle this." He found this conversation even harder than he thought it would be.

"Just come back and let's talk. Trent, you . . . you just have no idea how messed up things are now. Our divorce should be complete within a week or two, if you sign. But that's just *us!* The church is brokenhearted, our reputations are shot. I know *yours* is! Trent, how could you have done this? You stupid, stupid jerk!" She let out a wail.

"Natalie. Did you say our divorce is moving forward?"

"Yes, well, you told me to go forward with it, and I felt so deserted, so angry, I could think of no other option. You left me with no other choice, Trent! You just left me, Trent! Left me! Left fifteen years of marriage and a great job at a great church! I can't even believe it!" She began to sob again.

"Natalie, this is a difficult call for both—"

But she broke in, continuing her train of thought. "And I don't care, because I'm going to be just fine. This isn't hard for me. Oh, no, Trent. But *you.* I hope it *is* hard for you! You don't deserve a life anymore."

Now Trent wanted to cry out of sadness and a familiar frustration. He agreed with almost everything she was saying, and it hurt to hear her anger. Worse, he knew they wouldn't get anywhere. This conversation was a dead end—in fact, it wasn't even a conversation. Their discussions seemed to always turn this way, with him unable to get in a word edgewise. "Natalie."

"Don't you try and 'Natalie' me! I've been back here

with no idea what was going on, I've spent thousands of dollars on an investigator, and then you suddenly decide to send another one of your stupid notes through your stupid pastor friend in Alabama."

So she knew about that.

"Mom and I even went to Alabama when we got the first letter. Thought we could find you, you jerk! But no, just another clever trick you pulled!" Sobbing. "Who are you, anyway? Who does this kind of thing? Why?"

"Natalie, I'm sorr—"

"Don't you give me that! Just forget it! Don't call back. I can't take it."

And then the line went dead.

Suddenly Trent felt overwhelmed, like he'd never find his way. This part of his rebuilding blueprint wasn't going well—would the rest of it? He had wanted to talk to Nat tonight and say he was sorry and try to begin to do what he could to repair all of the damage he had caused. But of course she would be filled with rage and disgust. Of course she would need to vent on him. He had caused this, after all. Where would they go from here?

He sat alone on the deck of the ship in the dark of the night. But this time, no tears came. *Father, forgive me. Please forgive me, and through your grace, repair the damage I've done.*

Trent needed to get his mind somewhere besides his past, his old world. So he decided to call Nick and see how things in his new world were coming along. He might even leave the ship a week early, the day after tomorrow, and go back to work. He wanted something to do to occupy his mind, at least until a meeting with Natalie could be arranged, until it was time to revisit that part of his life.

"Hello, Nick, it's Trent. How are you?"

"Trent! Hey, I'm not sure. I mean, work is fine, and the family's good. But Trent, we need to talk. I'm glad you called. What have you done to get so many people looking for you? Trent, the *FBI* was asking about you today at the office. You'd better tell me what's up. What have you not told me?"

He was stunned. *The FBI?* "That . . . that has to be a mistake, Nick. The FBI?" Even as he said it, his throat went dry and he had to force himself to swallow. Fear and panic were strangling him.

"Yes, the FBI! It was them for sure. They wanted to know where you are. I told them you were on vacation. They asked how you got vacation time after working for a month. I told them the whole story you gave me—I was scared, man. They said they needed to question you regarding an investigation. Trent, you'd better come back and get in touch with them. In fact, I guess I can give you the number, and you can call them from there." Trent took the agent's cell number and said he'd call right away.

"Hey, listen." Nick's voice lowered, and Trent could tell he was getting serious. "I'm sure you don't have anything to hide. But I need to know if . . . if there's something I need to know. I have to think about my business and my family. You understand, right?" Trent gulped. Yes, he assured Nick, he did understand.

He knew from experience that dreaded calls set aside for later only became even more dreaded. So he decided to call the agent right then. It was nighttime, but not too late to make the call. He decided to stand by the railing of the boat, far from other passengers, and try to speak quietly. His fingers trembled and he forced himself to breathe evenly as the call connected.

"Milton here."

"Yes. Um, sir, this is—"

"You're going to have to speak up."

"Oh, sorry." He cleared his throat and spoke directly

into the mouthpiece. "Lieutenant Milton, this is Trent Atkins, and my boss told me—"

"Oh, yeah, Mr. Atkins. We need to talk to you. Where are you right now?"

"I'm on a cruise ship, heading back to San Diego. We are due to arrive day after tomorrow," Trent reported.

"You say a cruise ship? Hmm. Well, Mr. Atkins, plan on a welcoming party. Are you making any more stops on your way in?"

"No, sir, we are sailing until San Diego."

"Will you turn yourself in, Mr. Atkins?"

"Um, what? Yes, sir, sure. But am I going to be under arrest for something?" The fear was building.

"No, not for now. We just need to speak with you."

"O-okay. So, where will I find you?" Trent asked.

They made arrangements to meet on the dock. The agent told Trent he'd have to "ride downtown" for a little questioning. Was he saying that jokingly? What was happening?

Natalie had called Brandon right after her conversation with Trent. "He was *so* mean, Brandon!"

"Did he yell at you?"

"No, he just tried to sound all calm, like there was no big deal or anything. I mean, this is a big deal! He's such a jerk! I mean. . . . Oh, I just want to see him hurt, Brandon."

Brandon had been around hurting people enough to know that this kind of emotion revealed more fear than bravado. He knew that somewhere inside of this rage was a hurting person who felt betrayed. He sensed the danger of losing her again. It would take very little for her to turn into a begging little girl, wanting her husband back. He needed to act.

"Natalie. I know you are overwhelmed, but you need to talk this out. I don't care who sees us—I'm coming by the house to pick you up. I care about you too much to leave you alone right now." He was taking charge, and she would let him.

"Yes. OK. Let me fix my makeup. I'll meet you down at the corner by the pharmacy; I can hop in your car there. Thanks, Brandon. You are wonderful."

"Thirty minutes?"

"Forty-five. I'm a mess!" She let out a small laugh and sniffed it back again.

Trent lingered on the deck of the ship. He sat and watched the last clouds of a storm front slip away to reveal an amazing night sky. The breeze tossed his hair and the night air felt cool and fresh. Wind had been a powerful symbol in Trent's life. It always spoke to him of God's nearness. Yet the fear that gripped him would not subside. The thought crossed his mind that he could run even farther—how far were they from the coast right now? Could he swim for it? He realized that thought was ridiculous. He had to quit running.

He prayed the words of the mystic Julian of Norwich, words he often used to center himself. *All will be well, and all will be well, and all manner of things shall be well.* But Trent realized he was in one of those places where his faith was too weak to rally his emotions. Fear's cold, steely knife was laying his soul bare.

As he stood, he found himself wondering about just who Father Timothy was. And standing alone and facing the deep, he hoped that somehow, the mysterious priest was praying for him.

It was half past eleven that night when Brandon pulled up to where Natalie stood at the corner. She looked gorgeous. He ran around to the passenger door, put his arm around her back, and eased her into the seat.

As he slid back into the driver's seat and closed the door, she said, "Thank you for coming, Brandon. Thank you for caring. Thank you for being all I've ever . . . all I've ever wanted in a man." She leaned over and embraced him.

He stopped the car's slow pace and pulled over to the curb as she pulled his face toward his.

"Kiss me," she said.

And forgetting that they were in the town where they both lived and worked, and where many of the neighbors knew her and Trent, they did kiss.

"Take us somewhere to be alone, Brandon."

And he did.

When Trent finally made it back to his cabin, he found the common area of their suite empty. Kim's room was farther back, down a small corridor, and the door was closed—she must have retired for the evening. He quietly stepped into his restroom and changed into a pair of shorts and a T-shirt to sleep in. Grabbing his journal, he picked it up to write. But words wouldn't come. Where could he start? *Oh, God, help me.*

A few minutes later, he noticed a citrus perfume in the air. "Where have you been?" Kim inquired.

"Out trying to right my ship," Trent replied with a sigh.

"Did you?"

"No. I'm taking on water." As soon as the words left his mouth, he regretted the feigned lightness and attempt at humor. There was nothing light about his soul right now, only darkness.

"What's happening, Trent? Can I help? Do you want to talk?"

Trent found himself thinking of ways Kim could help. But those thoughts made him feel guilty. "No." The response came out in an angry tone.

Kim had never seen this side of Trent. She looked at him fearfully only for a second, then sat down across from him on a stuffed chair. "What's happened?"

Trent loved having Kim close; he felt comforted by her presence and drawn to her beauty. Yet he felt intimidated by the thought of telling her all that just happened. He began in a semi-sarcastic tone. "Well, for the first time in more than a month, I spoke with my wife. For the first time in a week, I spoke with Nick, who no longer trusts me. And for the first time in my life, I spoke with the FBI—and they want me for questioning. Otherwise, it was about like any other evening." He looked at her, and his straight face delivered the chilling words with a stab of fear.

Instantly Kim was back with her deceased husband, trying to untwist the knots he created with his half-truths. Had she been wrong about Trent? Was he just another untrustworthy man? She couldn't believe his words, but heard her taut voice scratch out the question, "FBI—what?"

"I don't know, Kim. They want to question me about something. The agent didn't seem too threatening or anything, but evidently my running has drawn their suspicion. The guy wants me to meet him when we disembark in San Diego, and then go downtown to talk with him." Trent looked at her as if he were hoping she could tell him this was no big deal—happens every day.

No such assurance came.

"Any idea . . . you have no idea what for?"

"None."

"Are you scared?"

"Yeah, I feel sick. He said he had checked my bank card numbers—and he had them all just right!" He looked at her with wide eyes as if to say, *What can this mean?* "No one knew those numbers. They were the accounts I started secretly as I planned my, um, escape." His words came with a staccato clip.

"Did he say they'd keep you? Are they going to arrest you?" The fear gripped both of them now. It owned the room. She was on the verge of tears.

"No, I don't think so. He said it would only take an hour, two at the most."

Kim felt she needed to switch the subject. "How did it go with Natalie?"

He looked her in the eyes and said, "She's charging through with the divorce. Only days away. Oh, man, I don't know whether to be relieved or sad." He dropped his head in his hands.

Kim wondered where she fit in Trent's words. Was he relieved because he might be free to pursue her now? Did he hope to move quickly into exploring this *thing* that was so powerful between them? She found herself looking at her left ring finger and wondering if Trent would soon make a claim on her. Yet echoes of the word *FBI* flashed memories of her last marriage before her. She cringed almost imperceptibly, tucking her hands beneath her thighs, protecting her empty ring finger. "What do you mean, Nick doesn't trust you?" she asked.

"Oh, he didn't say that. But what would you think, Kim, if an investigator *and* an FBI agent contacted you about an employee. 'Something's fishy here!'—that's what I'd think."

Kim leaned forward in her chair and stared at him. Her eyes held none of the warmth he was used to. "So Natalie is doing the divorce thing, and Nick has doubts about you. Well, Trent, I'd say that when you up and run across the country, and suspicious things are happening all around you, you might just expect some tough stuff like this to happen. You may have run to get away from trouble, but I don't see you landing anywhere comfortable without some tough sailing in the meantime." She paused for a second then added, "And here I am, supposed to feel sorry for you?"

Trent was startled by her words. She had been his one sure thing, his comfortable place. Was she turning on him? He tried to form a response and realized that all he wanted to do was plead with her to be here for him, to comfort him. Her next words cut his thoughts short before he could speak them.

"Listen, Trent. We've gotten pretty close over the past weeks. We've been very honest with each other. So I'm not going to be fake now that we've hit a tough spot. I know you need me to be here for you right now. Yes, you've had a hard day. But hold on a minute! Pull yourself outside of your own hurt and consider mine. *Listen* to what I'm feeling. I take time away from work to come out and be with you on this cruise— which *I* took the time and trouble to provide for us—and then hear this FBI stuff and you pouting because Natalie—whom you deserted—is doing what you asked her to and getting a divorce. For the first time, I see Trent caring more about Trent than me, or Nick, or Natalie, or *anyone*! Forgive me, but it's a little disconcerting to share a suite with a stranger."

Kim stood to leave. Trent dropped his head and said, "Kim, you're right. I'm sorry. It's been all about me here tonight."

Her arms folded across her chest, she sat back in front of him. "Listen, I understand. You are having a— " she paused to edit the expletive on her tongue, "—you are having a lousy day. You deserve an opportunity to vent, and I am glad to be the 'ventee.' But this is real life, and I'm ready to watch now just how you choose to mix your faith with this crisis. And I also want you to know that this is affecting *me*. All of it." She sat down and moved to the front of her chair, and putting her hands on his knees, she looked into his eyes. "I'm going to take a walk, and then I'd like to start over with this whole conversation. Sorry if I've been unfair. I guess I'm having flashbacks to some bad times in my life." Then she stepped out the door and into the night.

chapter 11

THE PARABLE OF
THE GYM

Trent's fear of rejection and feelings of being rejected ran deep. He dreaded Kim's return even as he longed for it. When she did step back into the room, their conversation was kind and brief. Both apologized sincerely, and both accepted, each feeling they had been the one in the wrong.

Kim mentioned that she felt really tired, and Trent bit at the opportunity to be alone and rest. Thinking he needed to blow off some steam with a good workout, he decided he'd check out the ship's onboard gym first thing tomorrow.

He felt strong. He'd done the first two sets with the dumbbells easily, and he was lifting more weight than usual. Walking to the bench press, he noticed that a healthy guy with shiny teeth and perfect hair had left a barbell already loaded with weights. It was quite a bit more weight than he usually would lift, but he was a monster today—he was sure he could handle it. Besides, there were plenty of people around to help if he got into trouble. And that guy—was he a pastor?—was nodding at him, encouraging him to go for it.

He sat on the bench and scooted beneath the bar, feeling confident. Taking a deep breath, he gripped the bar and lowered it to his chest. He blew out hard, hoisting the weights up with difficulty. But he did it. The next reps seemed easier, and he clanged the bar back onto the rack. He stood up to stretch, enjoying the admiring glances of those around, and noticed a hint of jealousy on the face of the pastor guy. He liked that.

He sat again, moved under the bar, and looking around, he noticed a growing audience in the workout room. Kim had come in and was watching proudly. Once again he took in a deep breath and hoisted the bar. But he could barely move it off the stand—somehow extra weight had been added. The bar came down hard, his arms unable to even slow its crushing weight. The weight on his chest pushed the air out of his lungs. He could not cry out. His eyes stared in terror and a vein throbbed in his neck as he realized that suddenly no one was near. He was alone, his legs flailing. The bar was crushing him, and his felt his ribs breaking. He pleaded with his useless muscles, "Push!"

Trent crashed from his bed, his legs kicking the chair over on himself. He thought he heard the echo of a shout. He was sweating. *A nightmare, only a bad dream! Oh, thank God.* He wondered if Kim heard the ruckus.

Trent's journal was lying facedown and open on the floor, having tumbled when he pushed at the nightstand during his fall. He picked it up and held it for a while, his thoughts spinning. It was as if a tangle inside his stomach—made up of fear, regret, and memories of his days as a pastor—was starting to unwind. Whatever was inside him, it wanted to be heard. It had to be heard. Soon he began to write.

The Parable of the Gym

There once was a teenage girl named Tammy who was morbidly obese. She had been embarrassed all her life by her size, her weight. She didn't like her body, and so—in keeping with the culture she lived in—she didn't like herself.

One day a healthy person asked Tammy to walk with her every day. She told her it helped her feel better, and she thought Tammy should try it too. When Tammy started losing weight, her healthy friend asked if she would read a book about how to be healthy, and then they could talk about it together. That day, Tammy decided to be healthy. She read the book regularly and began to eat better and walk more frequently.

Tammy slowly lost weight, and after a couple of years she was beautiful. Boys liked her and looked at her. Now she liked herself and how she felt, and so she went to college to learn how to help other girls learn to be healthy.

She studied diet trends and rules for healthy eating. She studied the human body and its systems. She bought magazines and collected books about health and diet. She learned that being thin is different from being in good shape. So Tammy started going to a gym and working out. She developed her muscles from head to toe. Soon Tammy looked even better, and she felt even better about herself.

When Tammy graduated from the university, it was time to go and help fat people get healthy. So Tammy got a job at a gym as a personal trainer. She was also a certified dietitian and taught classes on how to eat in a healthy way. She spent most of her days at work helping healthy people look stunning.

One day she ran an advertisement in the local paper for a new "Get Fit" class. Some obese people came. Tammy told them how she used to be obese and now she was happy and fit. They seemed motivated to be happy and fit too.

Trent paused and nibbled at the end of his pen, remembering how his ad for a new "How's Your Spiritual Fitness?" sermon series was run in the paper right next to a local fitness center's advertisement for a "Fitness 101" class.

But then they left her classroom and went to the workout room. She noticed how bad the obese people looked next to the buff people. The buff people noticed too, and the obese people could tell. They felt extremely uncomfortable huffing and puffing while walking slowly on a treadmill next to a guy who was sprinting on another machine and barely sweating. And as the class went on, it grew smaller and smaller each week—the number of obese people slowly dwindled.

[Being a pastor is like preparing to help people with a problem and then spending all your time with people who don't need you, who already agree with you on the problem's solution. You read the same books and share all the same beliefs with the faithful who come to your church. People who need your guidance don't feel comfortable being around those so confident in their own faith. To make matters worse, sometimes the church introduces required lifestyle expectations before the spiritually curious have found our Hope, and they fall away. As pastors, we can't be like the friend who helped Tammy start walking and get in shape, because church work keeps us busy, and our church friends wouldn't approve of us spending so much time with outsiders.]

Tammy didn't realize that the obese people weren't unmotivated; they were afraid. Most of them visited the gym with high hopes. They paid their membership dues with visions of wearing new, smaller clothes and enjoying new confidence, a brand-new life. But after a month or two, even after some improvement, they got tired of feeling out of place. Regulars could tell they were newcomers and had no confidence that they would ever really get thin and fit. The newcomers doubted it too.

Trent stopped writing and said a prayer for several friends. Their faces were playing like a movie before his closed eyes— people who took hold so well at his church at Baylor's Bend, who wore smiles for only so long, and then came up missing at services. Shaking his head, he resumed his writing with a new intensity.

Now, at first the newcomers were just quietly jealous of the committed gym people and health experts. They were jealous of their fitness and their clothing size; they were jealous that they could go to the beach and look good in a swimsuit.

But after a while they grew angry more than jealous. The people of the gym lobbied for laws against french fries. They wanted to add taxes to ice cream. They had bumper stickers, key chains, and T-shirts that advertised their gym, some of which hinted that obese people deserved their shorter lifespans. Others said things like "Honk if you love being fit and beautiful."

[The church in North America has lived past its days of having the admiration of those outside of it. Participants have cloistered themselves into their own church buildings and subculture. No one feels welcome coming in from the outside, and few are willing to fight their way past those social and cultural barriers. Church people have their own music, books, and magazines. Not to mention the way they condemn and threaten those outside of their "club" with antagonistic bumper stickers and T-shirts. One church near Baylor's Bend posted this message on their marquee during a heat wave: "'You think this is hot!' –God." Classy. Just imagine a spiritual seeker driving by that church to visit the grave of a loved one.]

Trent fought tears and a sudden urge to walk away from his journal and take a lap around the deck of the ship. He knew church people. He understood they had the best of intentions. From his local deacons to the staff at denominational headquarters, they meant well and were passionate about their faith. Yet what he was writing seemed so true. The church had distanced itself from those outside of it.

And wow, did those gyms compete with each other. To stay competitive, they needed lots of hunky instructors, the latest, trendiest exercise equipment, and the coolest and biggest facilities. Tammy's gym created a building program. They increased their dues for members, held bake sales, and sold all kinds of stuff—bars and shakes and drink mixes that really weren't healthy at all— to make money to get their new, bigger building and more high-tech equipment.

And once the building was done, they couldn't keep people away (fit people, that is). But Tammy was sorry to see that obese people didn't like the new gym any better than the old one—at least not for long.

People transferred their memberships from other smaller gyms in town, and the money flew in. Tammy got a raise. She had more people hiring her for personal training. Even her fit friends who worked at other gyms were jealous of her. But she had plenty of friends anyway—really healthy friends at her gym.

[Churches compete with other churches for members. They build expensive buildings, develop impressive "cutting edge" programs, and hire the sharpest up-and-coming staff available. They try to provide more than other churches so that people will transfer in.

Because of the expense of their buildings, staff, and

*programs, local churches have become as aggressive at
raising funds as TV churches. People who don't do church
realize this, and make no mistake, they talk about it with each
other.]*

Trent paused to remember a denominational workshop he'd
attended that confirmed his suspicions: the vast majority of
newcomers in churches have come from another church, not
from outside. He pondered the huge investments in buildings
and staff, and the resulting financial strain upon congregations,
all for the purpose of having the best place around.

*Soon Tammy's gym decided to franchise. This was
really cool. They would use some of their dues to build another
gym in a nearby town and find some people who needed to get
into shape. Tammy volunteered for the new position, hoping to
return to her earlier dreams of reaching unhealthy people.*

*So Tammy moved to a new town and helped open a new
gym. A percentage of the dues from the new gym had to go to
the first one, so that they could start more gyms, so that more
people could get fit. What a vision! But Tammy's gym couldn't
buy the equipment they needed for their gym to grow as big
as the first one. They simply couldn't afford it after sending so
much money back to the franchisor.*

*So a nearby competitor, with a nicer building and
better equipment, seemed to get all the thin people. Tammy did
find one slightly overweight and out of shape man and spent
lots of time training him. But when the man got in shape, his
healthy friends told him about all the advantages the bigger
gym in town offered, and so he transferred his membership!
Tammy knew that gym wouldn't give him the personal attention
she had, but off he went. She cried when she got the transfer
letter.*

Trent paused, remembering when he had served in smaller churches. He'd seen so very many young families, new to the faith, recruited into the megachurches down the road by friends who honestly believed that their bigger church was better.

Tammy had to keep a lot of books too. How many new memberships? How much money collected for classes and bake sales? What were the ages of all the new members? How many of them transferred from other gyms, and how many were newly healthy? It was overwhelming. But she knew that if her new gym grew big enough, she could afford to hire staff to keep all the records she had to submit.

Pretty soon, though, Tammy barely had time to work out herself. She missed walking on a treadmill. She remembered when she even used to walk outside! She started to miss ice cream. And that was when she knew that something needed to change.

One day, Tammy felt especially sad. She had become so busy with her gym work, and so competitive with other gyms, that she had lost her friends. She was lonely, and she started noticing something very strange. Even though she was surrounded by fit people, they didn't seem happy either. She noticed something else: the people who were not fit seemed happy. They went to parties and dances and got jobs and raises, and they seemed to like each other. They ate regular food and carried a few extra pounds, and they didn't compete with each other over who was the most fit, because they just liked to live.

Tammy began to think about quitting. She secretly dreamed of running away and hiding. She might even move to a state that hadn't taxed ice cream. Was she lost? Hopeless?

[I've heard that a researcher asked the following question to senior pastors in North America: "If you knew you could find another way to provide for your financial needs, would you leave the ministry?" More than half of the pastors said yes.

There comes a time when the joy is gone. We lose our sense of purpose, and people outside of the church culture start to seem better adjusted than those within. Even if half of pastors don't quit, many entertain fantasies of running. I've spoken with and counseled several of them. I just happened to take action on my fantasies.]

After Trent had recorded these things, he looked over what he'd written. He chuckled in places, then grimaced and felt regret in others. Why had he put up with this for so long? Why hadn't he been honest about these things when he was in a position to address them? What was it in him that was so hard-wired against confrontation?

His running was a poor way of dissenting to the status quo. He had a childish fit, and in the process perhaps he made a point. Now it was too late to lead change in Baylor's Bend. It was too late to impact the state of the larger church. The one brash statement made by his departure was the only one he'd have the opportunity to make. How much better it would have been if he had been bold enough to confront the monster before he'd run out of the room where it made him cower?

Reflecting further, he remembered how much he resented quitters who left his churches, and then he realized just how similar his departure from his congregation had been. Communication is a weak spot in the church, he concluded, and he'd learned so many habits and methods from the church. He, like so many angry laymen he'd known, would not openly disagree with how things were or invite friendly conversations about how things might need to change. No, he had acted in the fashion of so many who had left Baylor's Bend when something wasn't as they wished. He left in a fit, and demeaned them in his conversations after leaving.

Was Jesus a quitter? No. Did he have passionate disagreements with the religious establishment of his day? Yes. What did he do? He stood up against the wrong. He pointed out what was wrong. He prayed for the wrongdoers. Then he condemned those who wielded religious position and law against religious outsiders. Jesus stood his ground. And he was killed for it.

Lord Jesus Christ, son of God, have mercy on me, a sinner.

STAKING CLAIMS

After driving around for almost forty minutes, Brandon finally pulled into an all-night restaurant. "Let's grab a bite to eat."

Natalie considered asking him just to stay in the car while she got the food to go. The idea of cheating, of breaking her vows before the divorce was final, revolted her. She didn't even know how the finality of divorce would affect her feelings about being with another man. All the same, she decided she would ask Brandon to find them a room that night. She would shatter the promise she'd made at the altar and leave it behind in this city, so many miles away from Trent Atkins—the man to whom she'd first yielded her heart and soul, and the man who had forsaken her so completely.

Brandon opened her car door and stood waiting. And as they walked up the sidewalk, past a neon sign that read "Open 24 hours," she gained courage. While sharing a cheeseburger and fries, they decided where they would go next. That decision would change the rest of their lives. He dropped her in front of her mother's home just before five in the morning. She walked up to the door with staggering, distracted steps, fighting tears and feeling very, very old.

"Bishop Phillips, this is Emma Lawrence, Natalie Atkins's mother."

"Yes," the bishop said.

"Natalie left last night. She was gone until early this morning. Well, I finally just fell asleep, so I don't know how late she got in. But I think she got in a car with one of the staff members from Baylor's Bend—Brandon Tyler. I don't know what to do."

"Well, are you assuming she's all right?" he asked.

"Yes, I'm sure she is. But I'm just concerned, you know, about her soul."

He took a breath. "Ask her to give me a call, would you?"

"Yes. Thank you, Bishop." Then she added, "This whole thing is just a mess."

"It certainly is that, Mrs. Lawrence, it certainly is that. Now, you take care." And with that he disconnected.

Kim finally gave up waiting on Trent to get up. She quietly stepped into the room where he was sleeping and found his journal. He'd laid a note across the pages of the opened book: *Kim, feel free to read the last few pages.*

While reading his heartfelt handwriting, she noticed that moist drops—teardrops, she assumed—had diluted and smeared some of the ink. After reading, she sat back in the chair and watched him sleep so innocently. Never had she been around a man who treated her so kindly, so gently. He'd even shared a suite with her, yet there he lay, sleeping alone—on purpose.

As Trent compared himself to "Tammy," she finally began to grasp his agony, an agony that had made him run. He loved people, but he'd grown to hate his job. Instead of loving people and expressing to others in his beautiful way how to understand Jesus, he was running a company. He was misplaced.

Kim knew she had already learned so much from Trent about the God of love, the God who was Jesus. And she wanted to know more. But she identified completely with the people in the parable who wanted nothing to do with the gym. She was one of them.

She understood. Trent wanted to share the peace he knew in Jesus. And he didn't want to hide behind corporate walls of such a mistrusted "company" in order to share Life.

And this Jesus, this one Trent had taught to her, was not hidden away in some church—or "gym," as the parable said. He was right out in front in Trent's life, ready to love or serve or care for whoever needed him. He was loyal and faithful to a fault.

Kim had to admit that Trent himself attracted her. She wanted to be around him. She didn't want him to move back to his old city, his old life. And even though she wanted him to do what he needed to do—what was best for him—she held on to hope that one day they would be together, just the two of them together with no outside interference. She didn't want to let go of that hope. And for now, as she sat so early on this new day looking at him as he slept, she would hold on.

And what was the FBI thing about? *This* man sleeping in front of her could not be guilty of anything. She felt sure of it. If he was, he'd blurt it out, confess it with tears. He was too real, too tender to hide dark secrets. Such secrets would shatter him.

"Trent," she whispered. "Trent, I'm going out to get some breakfast." Not sure he had heard her, she patted the key card in her pocket and stepped out into the bright new morning.

When Natalie got up, her mother told her that Bishop Phillips needed her to call. "What does he want? Do you know?" Natalie asked.

"No. He just wants you to call."

Natalie couldn't have thought of a worse time to face the bishop. She decided to put on her cheery voice and call him anyway. Perhaps he had a new letter or something to tell her about.

Once they'd exchanged formalities, he asked, "Natalie, are you doing all right?"

"Oh, yes, just fine." She used her finest fake, syrupy-sweet, bright and cheery voice. Years of living in the fishbowl of ministry had honed it to perfection.

"Well, I just wanted to check. When I spoke with your mother this morning, she seemed a little concerned about you, and I thought I should check up on you. That's all."

Natalie, her eyes wide, let out a huge, yet quiet sigh of relief. "Oh, thank you, Bishop Phillips. You have been so kind through this horrible ordeal." Her voice raised even a degree higher; she thought it sounded like a children's pastor's.

"Have you thought of how you'd like to handle your first conversation with Trent?" the bishop asked.

"No . . . well, yes, of course. I just can't seem to decide what to do. Could you give me your opinion on that, Bishop?"

"I've done some thinking and checking with a friend or two in the counseling business. They seem to think it would be good for each of you to speak with your own counselor privately before you meet face to face. Then you could come together, either with the counselors present, or with a neutral party. The neutral party could be me or another individual with whom you'd feel comfortable," he said. After a pause, he asked, "Does that make sense to you, Natalie?"

"Yes. I think so. At least, I think he needs to see a counselor first. He needs to know how badly he has hurt a lot of people. I'm not just talking about me, of course."

"Of course," he said. "But I do believe you both could benefit from the wisdom of an outside intermediary. Now, I do have funds available to cover all of the costs of these professionals."

"Well, I guess I just don't like the implication that *I* need a professional, that I need to see a counselor. I mean, here I am sitting all alone because of the stupid, silly decisions *he* has made. I mean, *I'm* the normal one here!"

"Yes, but when a person has been injured by another *physically*, we don't deny the victim first aid, do we? It should be the same way spiritually and emotionally. We simply want to offer you the best care we can."

"No, I guess you're right. It wouldn't hurt me to be heard."

Soon it was settled. Trent and Natalie would meet separately with two counselors, and then they would all talk together.

Natalie felt she couldn't say no. The bishop had been so kind—and maybe pushed a right button or two. But she couldn't help but wonder what this resistance was in her heart. Was it that she didn't want to try with Trent any longer? Was she eager to move on with Brandon? Or was there something left between her and Trent? Was she frightened that something might spark between them? She sighed. It didn't matter. It would all be over soon. She'd deal with this the way she'd dealt with everything: by picking herself up and moving on.

The last full day of the cruise was difficult for Trent. No matter how hard he tried to shake the thought of questioning by the FBI, he couldn't help but worry. This was a first. He had never been near any trouble.

Kim tried to give him all the distance he needed, but realized that he cheered up when she was with him. She spent much of the day reminding him of their walks on the beach or of how much Nick liked his work. She asked him to tell her more about his work life as a pastor and showed a genuine interest in his answers.

After dinner that night, she asked Trent if he would like to dance. A band was playing, and the night breeze and golden sunset made the evening perfect. Trent said he'd never danced anything but a slow dance. "That's just what I'd hoped for," she told him. Actually, she believed it was just what he needed. After a day of verbal comforting, she was sure that being held by someone who cared would soothe him.

Trent took such comfort from the music and the night. Having Kim's arms around his back and neck felt so perfect. She had been such a friend to him since their last talk on the beach, the night they realized they needed to drop the romantic side of their friendship. Yet as they danced, he realized she felt like more than a friend to him. This felt good—too good.

As they returned to their suite, he knew he needed to ask her to go on back to her room and leave him. But Trent ached for company—Kim's company. He wanted to have this beautiful woman holding him and telling him everything would be all right. And before he could speak a word, she stepped into his room and squared the two stuffed chairs face to face.

She sat down in one, and pointed to the other. *Well*, he thought, taking a seat, *at least she won't be holding me.* But as she slipped out of her sandals, she rested her legs on his chair, to his left side. He found himself doing the same, placing his feet up by her side, resting on her chair.

He was falling. And this was no time to be falling. He didn't have the protection of prying eyes. He didn't have the protection of separate rooms. Where was this going? What was he doing?

As his head spun with these questions, she asked,

"Trent, when you go back . . . you know, to Illinois . . . when you go back there, do you think you and Natalie will get back together?"

"I just don't know, Kim. But I can't feel right about anything that lies ahead unless I've given my marriage to Natalie a genuine opportunity to recover."

"I see," she said.

Silence.

"Trent."

"Yeah."

"I've never been around a man like you. I mean, I guess I've never been around a Christian. You treat me with such respect. Here we are, all alone in this room. And I trust you to treat me well. I'm not thinking about how to fend you off." She paused, then added, "I mean, I can tell that you have the needs of a man, that you do have desires, but. . . . " She didn't know what else to say.

"If only you knew how difficult this is for me right now. Kim, you are so beautiful. I can't quit looking at you. I can't quit wanting you, but I know I just can't take this any further." He looked away from her. "I'm sorry, I'm not making sense."

"Oh, no! You're making all kinds of sense. You are complimenting me . . . thank you. And you are normal. And so am I. And *I* want *you*." She put her feet back on the floor and Trent followed suit. She scooted her chair until their knees touched. She turned around and squeezed in next to him in his chair. Then she reached her arms around his back and pulled him close. She held his gaze with her beautiful eyes and said, "And I need you."

And then they kissed. Trent saw his bed from the corner of his eye and knew he was nearing disaster. *I can't stand up to anyone*—he remembered journaling that thought. But he didn't want to stand up to this. He wanted to relax into this wonderful moment, go to sleep in this woman's arms and never get up. And then a new thought invaded his mind: *bloody bones.* He sat up, kissed Kim tenderly on her forehead, and switched to the opposing chair.

"Kim. I'm afraid I'm feeling things for you right now that I shouldn't. I find myself hoping that you can be my future, that you can be my healing and my love and my life. But that just can't happen right now. I can't go building my life on lies again. If you and I can ever share a life, it will have to be built on a better foundation than passion and these wonderful feelings we have."

Kim brushed back her hair and looked at Trent, who now sat across from her. Her eyes were misty, and her cheeks flushed with what looked like embarrassment.

Trent said to her, "You have surrounded me with support and love and care all day long. You have held me in my darkest moments. You have offered me hope and comfort. Thank you." He paused. "Right now I just want to tell you that I love you. And I do love you, but not as a wife. We aren't there yet. We may never be. And so, according to the foundations and values that make sense for me, I can't take you now as if you were my wife. And believe me, I am so very sorry."

Kim looked stunned. He assumed that finally she thought he was just another religious fundamentalist lunatic. But then she spoke. "You are wonderful—amazing! I understand. And you need to know that I'm cheering for a happy ending for *us*! And if there is one, I will bring you to this very boat for a honeymoon. And I'll pray for that day until it comes." She stopped and wiped a tear. "And if it doesn't, I'll always have these memories. And with those memories I'll carry hope that there really is Love—Love who lives in people and loves through them."

He dropped his head, feeling so grateful for being rescued by memories of Father Timothy—and at the same time wishing he were able to sleep in this woman's arms tonight and for the rest of his life. But life, he thought, was more than comfort, more than passions fulfilled. It must be built on something solid, and his faith gave him a foundation that was making more sense every moment.

Kim broke the brief silence. "Trent."

"Yeah, sorry, just thinking."

"No, that's okay—me too. Trent, could you pray for us, or do what you usually do quietly—out loud instead? You know, for me to hear too?"

And he did. Then she thanked him and left for her room.

Brandon liked the idea of Natalie having a counselor with her when she met with Trent. He didn't want them alone, where weak passions could overcome her new life. However, he had to fight the urge to coach her about questions that might come up about the times he had spent with her since Trent left. That could wait.

The newspaper continued to offer no news regarding the Saint John's case. And in Brandon's opinion, no news had to be good news. There were apparently no suspects and no leads besides "the mysterious disappearance of a man who fled the state on the afternoon of the murder." He couldn't help but smile at the thought of a future headline: the *Reverend* Atkins arrested for the murder of a helpless hospital patient. That would ruin Trent's reputation forever. And Brandon might even get some cash for being interviewed on a twenty-four-hour news show.

Memories of his times with Natalie sent shivers of delight through him. He felt like a teenager again as he dreamed of the date he'd planned for the weekend: a nighttime dinner cruise on Lake Michigan. Things were getting good, very good indeed.

Trent woke early the next morning. His first thought was to go to Kim's room for a morning hug. Bad idea. So he moved on. Visiting the breakfast bar, he decided he would spend his morning doing a bit more journaling, taking a quick jog on a treadmill, and if he could schedule it, getting a haircut before his dreaded meeting with the FBI agent.

Sitting in his now familiar deck chair and enjoying the morning coffee, Trent began to write some thoughts for Natalie.

> *Natalie,*
>
> *From the beginning, Natalie, we have spoken of our love as a commitment. We promised—even vowed—that no matter what feelings might someday arise, we would be true to our pledge. We were wisely counseled before our marriage to see challenges as opportunities for growth. We were told that saying "I love you" means promising to work through come what may in order to stay the course of a lifetime marriage.*
>
> *I have already written and spoken to you of my undying regrets about leaving you. I was so wrong to do that. Please, however, let me apologize once again. There is no excuse for what I have put you through.*
>
> *Now I need to be fully honest. The rift I allowed to develop between us is real. I have long been aware that your feelings for me are largely gone. I must say that on the emotional level, I have no romantic longing for you. But as I again think back to our pre-marriage counseling, I remember the advice that we should see "I love you" as a choice, not a feeling. So in the spirit*

of that promise, that commitment of love, I have kept myself for you. I belong to you by the vows I have made.

Obviously, my desertion was an abusive and devastating emotional blow to you and everyone else to whom I had promised my devotion. That alone could be enough reason for you to give up on me. However, I want you to know that my desertion has not led me to commit any physical act of adultery. And in this crazy world I've created, that is one thing that gives me hope that I might be able to rescue the marriage I have otherwise allowed to die.

Nat, I have no idea how you will respond to this. I only need to say that I am willing to enter a counseling relationship to see if our promises continue to hold any merit. I have done more than my share to crush them. I pray that at least I will someday know your forgiveness and God's.

Trent

Trent folded the note and tucked it into his journal. He then dashed to an Internet café aboard the ship and typed it, then e-mailed it to Natalie, copying Bishop Phillips and giving him the go-ahead to send it to any marriage counselor the bishop might choose. Then he packed his things and hurried to make his 10:45 haircut.

He had pictured all kinds of dramatic TV-style arrest scenarios. But what happened at the harbor was anything but dramatic to the casual observer. In fact, Trent imagined that his meeting with the FBI agent looked more like two new friends finding one another and making introductions. But the drama was real. He had never been involved on this end of a legal issue, and he didn't like it.

The ride downtown was quiet. Lieutenant Milton looked and acted like every crime-drama stereotype. He wore a tired shirt with an out-of-date tie over his broad chest. He was tall, and if his title wasn't intimidating enough, his quiet, focused demeanor did the trick. By the time they reached the FBI offices, Trent needed the restroom. No problem. The agents would wait.

They started with some introductory information and reminders: Trent was welcome to have an attorney present; he was not under arrest and was speaking to them only voluntarily. Whatever this was about, he figured it was a good idea to be as helpful as possible.

The interrogation was cordial, but maintained a steady, intense rhythm. Trent answered questions about his trip west—when he bought the ticket, where he got the money, and why the sudden exodus. He got the idea they thought maybe he was running from something besides life in general. They kept circling around the questions of what time he'd left the Jenkins family at the hospital and what time he'd arrived at the airport.

The officers seemed especially interested in the timing of his escape. They asked when he had used the bank cards and when he'd left the hospital.

After he responded to those questions, the three officers stepped to another table in the interrogation room and talked. Trent heard one of them say, "Look at this. The Jenkins surgery wasn't over until 10:55. Reverend Atkins stayed until he could see her after the recovery room, which wasn't until 12:30. He had to be there until at least 12:40. So his story about taking the CTA from the hospital on Michigan Avenue fits seamlessly with the last use of his old cell. The text message was at 1:13, he was into the bank machines by a few minutes after that, and then he made the two calls at 1:39 and 1:41."

Another voice said, "And our victim's earliest time of

death wasn't until 2:00. I mean, the coroner's best guess was 2:30 or later, and they tried to revive her when they found her just moments after that."

The lieutenant spoke next, in a whisper: "Let me look at that timeline again." A few seconds later, he moved back to Trent's table.

"Mr. Atkins, your story seems to work with the facts." He gave a reassuring smile.

"I plan to go back to the Midwest soon. Is that going to be a problem?" Trent asked.

"Not at all. I have your cell number." Lieutenant Milton shook Trent's hand and walked him to the door. "I don't think you have anything to worry about here, Reverend Atkins."

Brandon cursed under his breath. The evening news had a breaking story about another identical molestation and murder at Saint John's earlier that afternoon. Unless Trent had come back for another murder—and Brandon knew better—he was off the hook.

Kim was waiting by a park bench. The feeling of relief that swept over Trent as he walked toward her was intoxicating. He took in her beauty and greeted her. "Glad that's over!"

He explained everything that happened, including the whispered timeline he had overheard. Somehow his rapid escape from Chicago had raised their suspicion. There had been a crime that afternoon, and it sounded like a murder!

She told him that Nick and Allie were planning to meet them for a picnic dinner on the harbor. He could only smile and chatter about how good it felt to have the dreaded and mysterious appointment behind him. Kim could only listen and think about how happy she was to be with this man for the rest of the day.

That night Trent called Bishop Phillips, and they made arrangements for a meeting between Trent, the bishop, and Natalie the following Wednesday morning at the bishop's office. A counselor would meet with each of them on Tuesday night. The bishop wanted Trent to send whatever journaling he was willing to share about his reasons for escape. He also agreed to print the letter Trent had written to Natalie that morning and share it with the counselors.

Funny, Trent thought as they finished their call. *The bishop seems very understanding. Not vindictive or even professionally distant. He even said this wasn't the first time he'd seen this happen.* As he fell off to sleep, Trent didn't feel quite so alone as he had before the phone call.

Natalie called Brandon with the news of next week's appointments. He was glad to hear her saying the right things. She would just get through it. She didn't have any feelings of love for Trent any longer, but she had to participate in the sessions. It was all formality at this point. She had even told the bishop as much.

He couldn't resist telling her he thought she should leave him out of the conversations with the counselor and Trent. She assured him she wasn't stupid. He assured her he knew that. She wasn't sure he meant it. Brandon always felt the need to coach her.

Trent had worn nothing but jeans and shorts since his move west. He had brought one pair of khakis with him, but they were at least a size too large now. So he decided to go shopping for something semi-casual to wear to his meetings back east.

Kim accompanied him after work on Monday evening. He insisted on going to a secondhand shop. Trying on a pair of pants with a thirty-four-inch waist caused him to beam with pride. "Hey, these are a full size smaller than my usual!" He showed how much extra room he had left inside these smaller pants by placing both of his hands into the waistband.

"You need to start eating again!" Kim said. "But truly, I think you look perfect. How much are those?"

"Four bucks!" he laughed.

"Now that's a deal."

They picked out two shirts that matched and left the store after paying eleven dollars and change to the cashier. Trent said, "I've always wanted to get my clothes from a place like that. Seems like a good way to recycle and be frugal at the same time." Trent's wardrobe had always demanded a professional look. New clothing, starched shirts, and trendy ties had been his norm.

"I'm going to miss you," she said.

"Yeah, I'll miss you too. But the Shoemakers have said I can keep the place until I know what my future looks like." Then he turned and said, "Kim, I think you know my thoughts about being here, about being around you. But I really have to try and make things work out back in Illinois. I'd like to share a letter I sent from the cruise. It's for Natalie, and I sent it to the counselors who will be working with us. You deserve to know the whole picture."

They paused near a bus stop, and he handed her the handwritten copy of the letter.

He stepped away as she sat down on a bench to read. He couldn't resist watching her for clues of reaction. She wiped tears, and with her face lowered, she held the letter back out to Trent. "I'm sorry," she said. "I just don't know how to act or feel. Well, I know how I feel. I'm just not used to being around someone who has higher values than what he is feeling."

Trent could only stand and wonder what his faith—*his* faith—had gotten him into now.

Kim looked up at him and stood. "Most people want to

be happy. You want to be honest. Most people want to feel good. You want to feel . . . to feel true. Most people . . . most people run from person to person, or drug to drug, seeking some kind of lasting happiness. And you . . . you think happiness is in some deep principle or something." She looked away. "And I hate it. And I love you for it. You might as well know—and if you think it's a decision more than a feeling, that's fine—but I love you. I do. And I'm willing to wait as long as it takes for you to find out what you need to know about the two of you . . . about Natalie."

She turned once again toward him and continued. "And I won't call you or e-mail or write or try to keep any communication going while you're there. I'm letting you go. And I need you to do the same. You can't contact me. You have to run this path to its end. And at the end, let me know what the two of you have decided. I'll be OK either way."

They were quiet as the weight of Kim's words settled into them.

"Wow. I didn't want to hear that 'no communication' thing. You're right, though. I don't like it either. But I'm either giving my vows a chance or I'm not. And my renewed commitment to this life of truth demands that I do. Thank you, Kim. You are one of the most authentic people I have ever known." He became lost in thought, then said, "I guess I ought to get you home."

They said nothing as they rode back to her apartment and said simple, tearful good-byes. When they parted, he gave her only an awkward pat on her shoulder.

chapter 13

OLD WOUNDS

The bishop had found counselors to meet with Natalie and Trent. They would first meet with the counselors individually, and then see each other for the first time, with the two counselors and the bishop present, the next morning.

Natalie showed up a little early for the Tuesday evening meeting and met her counselor in the waiting area of Bishop Phillips's office. Cyndi Andrews was petite with premature streaks of gray—which she made no effort to conceal in her bobbed blond hair. She was attractive in an earthy, academic way and friendly, but very professional. Natalie could tell she was good at her job. Cyndi invited her to a small meeting room where they could speak privately. After introductions and some general background questions for Natalie, Miss Andrews got down to business.

"Before we even begin with this process, I'd like to know, Natalie, just what you think. Where are you with Trent? Do you have hopes, feelings, doubts, or what? Give me an initial reading. Of course, this is all strictly confidential."

Natalie looked her in the eyes. She wanted to be real— no acting—and she made the quick decision that she could be honest with this woman.

"I truly think I'm over it, Miss Andrews."

"Call me Cyndi, but go on, please. Over what?"

"We've been like roommates—at best, tolerable friends—for *years*. There have been few indications that we were husband and wife, even . . . well, even . . ."

"In the bedroom?" the counselor finished.

"Yes. I mean, that's been dead for at least a few years now. We shared a place, and we played the role of pastor and wife."

"What role was that?"

"You know. Love everyone, smile, act as if everything is just perfect. Then there was being strong for those in crisis, which sometimes seemed like just about everyone. And we had to be wise about things we had no idea how to handle, like what to do when your teenager thinks she's gay, or how to respond when you think your mother is having an affair, or when your husband is hiding a drug habit, or . . . well, you know. We just had to know it all, or act as if we did. It's just the way it is." Natalie sighed.

"That sounds like a pretty heavy weight."

"Yeah, I guess. I never really minded. But Trent heard a lot more than I did, and he never seemed to be able to let it go. He talked about work and people's problems and the next major project at the church all the time. I really do mean *all* the time."

"You were able to leave the stresses behind?"

"Yes. I know that people have problems, churches have problems, and when you combine the two, those are *big* problems. But when you leave work, you have to leave work. Listen to music, read a book that takes you away, or whatever. He could just never do that."

"What kind of guy is Trent?"

"Weak. He let people abuse him and he would never tell them it made him angry. Instead, he would hold it in and then let it loose on me."

"Did he abuse you?"

"Only if you call running away for a month with no way to call or contact him abuse." Natalie said. "Sorry. No, he never physically abused me. Silent treatment? Yes. Spilling all of his stress out at me? Complaining to me about all the stuff he had to decide and who was mad at him? Oh, yes! And when I shut that out and quit listening . . . it was over."

"When did that happen, Natalie?"

"Shortly after we moved to Baylor's Bend. We were both so excited about the opportunity when we moved here. It was such a large church, and it gave us more prestige and a livable salary. But we hadn't counted on the multiplication of stress. Trent started to stress out, and I remember the time when I just felt like I couldn't . . . I wouldn't take it anymore. So I quit listening. When he'd tell me about a problem on a committee or whatever, I'd just change the subject. 'How much *more* do you get paid here than at our last church?' I'd ask, trying to remind him of the benefits of a larger church ministry."

"And how did he respond, Natalie?"

"After a while, when he knew I wasn't going to listen anymore, it was like he just left. He didn't talk to me for long periods of time. Then he'd apologize and admit it was his fault and say he'd try to do better. But before long he'd start to bellyache and I'd ask him how he liked his *new* car, and we'd be back into a tiff. Finally, he quit talking to me about anything. That's when we just started role playing. And that was the holding pattern we entered a long time ago."

Cyndi Andrews noticed that while there was regret in Natalie's voice, she showed no sign of tears or sadness. It was all matter-of-fact. On her notepad, she wrote the word "over" and underlined it. If the letter she'd read from Trent Atkins accurately indicated a willingness to try, then he probably held unrealistic confidence in the vows the two had taken—vows they had not known how to keep when the stresses of ministry took hold. She had seen the same pattern far too often, couples with wonderful marriages running into ministry without a single clue of how big a toll the stress would ring up.

In Cyndi's opinion, Natalie had handled Trent's difficulties the only way she knew how. Hers was the "you've got to grow up and deal with it" mentality. Trent's was the "avoid conflict" plan. Rather than seeking guidance and counsel when they faced the wall, they hid behind the mask of marital bliss and slowly died behind the walls of a parsonage. And they had both ended up right where the problem had started: she had given up on Trent ever growing up and dealing with difficulties, and Trent had run from Natalie, church stress, and his career.

Cyndi's report left little hope for any reconciliation after tomorrow morning's meeting, the one that would bring Natalie and Trent back together.

Jeff Jones and Trent were to arrive at the bishop's office fifteen minutes after Natalie and Cyndi—to avoid any unnecessary confrontation before the next morning. Both Trent and Natalie needed the opportunity to meet with their respective counselors before they came together. Jeff greeted Trent as they walked up to the front steps. Trent liked him immediately. He was a youngish post-graduate type with kind eyes. He wore wire-rim glasses and trendy shoes.

They made their way to another meeting room. Trent couldn't help but catch a glimpse of the back of Natalie's head as he sneaked a peek in the other room while passing by. "That's her," he said to Jeff. "Wow, that's kind of weird. I haven't seen her for a little over a month."

"Do you miss her?" Jeff asked as they sat down in their private room and closed the door behind them.

Trent was quiet for a minute. "Miss her. . . . I don't

know."

"What are you feeling right now, Trent?"

"Regret."

"Say more."

"I've hurt her. I'm not even talking about this stunt. Sometimes I'm not so sure she even misses me. But over the last few years, I've hurt—damaged, even—a good person. Regret is what I feel . . . remorse," Trent said.

"How have you hurt her?"

"It's a long story."

"Let's begin."

"Silence. Acting like she didn't exist. Pretending I could live without anyone, and doing it, and wearing rage around the house like armor," Trent said.

"Why the silence, Trent? Why acting like she didn't exist?"

"Anger."

"About what?"

"Stuff. I didn't like my job anymore. I hated it. Well, parts I liked. I liked being with people and teaching on Sundays and all. But the longer I was here, in this bigger church with bigger problems and more hassles, I thought I might die."

"Do you mean you were sick?"

"Sometimes. I remember feeling so angry or alone that I would get weak and dizzy. I didn't know if I could get out of bed some mornings, and sometimes I closed my office door and slept in the afternoon. I would have horrible thoughts flash through my mind. Things like car wrecks with loved ones or me involved—very vivid imaginations of broken or severed limbs. Or if I'd see a spot on the side of the road, I'd imagine it was my blood. I'd have to shake myself out of it."

"Go on."

"Once I got so sick—so depressed. It was a couple of years ago. I asked the elders if they could get someone to preach

155

for me and let me have a couple of weeks away. They didn't like it, and they let me know. But Bishop Phillips told them they should give me the time, so they did. Natalie wouldn't go with me. Said I was weak, a wimp . . . a baby. It made her sick, she said.

"So, I went camping by myself. I just cried for several days. I couldn't eat, I couldn't sleep at night. I thought I was going crazy. Then a psychologist who was camping with his family nearby talked to me about stress. I spent some time with him, and he said he thought I might be suffering from a major depression and bordering on burnout. It helped me to have a name for what I felt. At least it wasn't some freak, chronic illness.

"He gave me a few tips. 'Fake it till you make it,' he said. He explained what he meant, that some things I could get away without doing. I could put less time into sermons, for instance, and no one would notice. And after a couple of days with me, he said I needed to get out of ministry. It just didn't suit me, and I couldn't be my real self *and* a pastor at the same time. I laughed and told him that I'd often thought I'd have to choose between being a Christian and being a pastor."

"So you planned your escape?" Jeff asked.

"No, not yet. I worked up the courage to tell Natalie that I'd decided to quit. I knew she wouldn't like it, but I had no idea how she'd react. The depression diagnosis didn't impress her—she really would have died if she'd known about the anti-depressants my doctor started giving me from his sample stash. When I told her I needed to take some time to deal with all this, she told me to grow up. She said being a pastor was what God called me to do, and that no shrink had any business crossing into that territory."

Trent started to weep. "*That's* when I started to plan my escape. And Jeff, the dream of running kept me alive. I was so lost, I didn't even think of the effects it would have on other people. All I could do was hold my breath and stay underwater until my day of liberation came. And then I surfaced with a gasp and ran."

Trent laid his head on the table in front of him and began to sob. "I've hurt so many people," he said through his pain.

"And all of them are still alive and breathing today, Trent. You probably overestimate the effect your life has on the lives of those around you. It's an occupational hazard."

They were quiet for a while. Trent used a few Kleenex to dry his eyes and blow his nose, and Jeff just let his last words settle in.

"I admired your letter, Trent. I do even more now that I've heard your story. And yes, I feel badly for Natalie. She has endured a great deal, as have you. But Trent, I feel terribly sad for you. You have shouldered an unbelievable weight all alone. And that has to stop. You are worth so much more than you give yourself credit for. You are a wonderful person—and that's according to just about everyone I've interviewed." Jeff sat back and let his words sink in once again.

The room buzzed with an odd mix of emotion. Jeff could sense that Trent was relieved, yet he also sensed unbearable sadness. And this was sadness that had gathered and festered for years. Here was a tender man—maybe a bit too tender to face the rigors of a senior pastorate. Trent was a lover, a giver, but not a man to be in charge. Trent's story, however, was not new to Jeff.

He saw it all the time: idealistic youth invited into the adventure of ministry, only to find themselves driving a huge organization from behind a desk, a position for which they are not prepared, facing persecution from an entire congregation of bosses. Trent was another victim of false advertising.

Trent's cell phone broke the silence. He'd meant to turn it off when he walked in, but got distracted.

"Go ahead and answer if it's important, Trent."

"Hello?"

"Lieutenant Milton from the FBI here, Trent. This a bad time?"

"Uh, no, not unless it's going to take a while."

"No, Reverend, it won't. Hey, we want to thank you for your cooperation. You are no longer a person of interest to us in this case. But you were a breath of fresh air to talk with. Thanks for your honesty and, well, integrity. Just don't see much of that in my job. Have a great evening."

"You too. Thank you, sir!"

Jeff could see the ease of tension on Trent's face as he finished the telephone conversation. "You look relieved."

"Big time," Trent answered. "That's one less thing to have on my mind."

"Why don't you get back to your hotel room and rest up for tomorrow, Trent?" Jeff suggested. He stood and led him to the door. Making sure Natalie and Cyndi's counseling room was vacant, he motioned that it was safe for Trent to step into the hallway. "I'll see you tomorrow morning. And don't worry, Trent. I think things will go well."

Kim hurried to Aunt Jo Anna's place as soon she got word. "How is she?" she asked as she stepped quietly through the open door.

Jenna, wiping tears, could only shake her head.

They walked arm in arm into Aunt Jo's room. She was still conscious, but they could see her pain. "Just hit me all of a sudden," she whispered to Kim. "Doctors say I'm not done, but the way I feel, being done might not be so bad."

"I love you, Aunt Jo," Kim said.

"Where's that good-lookin' Trent?" Jo Anna murmured. She managed to twist a smile onto her face.

"He's back in Illinois. Had some family business to

take care of."

That was enough explanation for Jo Anna. "Good kid, that Trent."

"Yeah, good kid," Kim agreed and smiled.

Jenna laid her head on Kim's shoulder. "Good man," Jenna said.

Kim wished Trent were there.

Nick's business missed Trent. His crew especially missed his leadership. Nick called Trent at 10:00 California time on Tuesday evening. He told him how much they missed him, but assured him they wanted him to do what he needed to do. Trent thanked him and went back to sleep, wondering if Nick had ever heard of time zones.

Jeff Jones and Cyndi Andrews met an hour before the meeting the next morning. They shared their stories. Stereotypical case, they agreed. Cyndi asked Jeff about Trent. After talking to Natalie and reading the letter Trent had written about commitment and vows and trying again, she joked that she couldn't wait to meet this guy. Either he had a serious issue with boundaries or was a genuinely kind man.

Jeff assured her of his opinion. "This is a good man. Broken, but good."

"I think Natalie is finished, Jeff. She's too far gone," Cyndi said.

"Yeah, I'm with you. It seems to me that Trent's hopes are noble, but not likely. In fact, even if he wants to do the right thing and stay in his marriage, I think deep down inside he'd like to just start over. I think that's why he left in the first place, and I think his leaving was the first bold and important step he took to reclaim his own life. In my opinion, these two need to leave well enough alone," he said.

"And leave each other alone," Cyndi agreed.

They briefed Bishop Phillips during the final thirty minutes before the planned gathering. The bishop wanted to discuss Trent's future ministry options, whether or not their marriage worked out. But Jeff expressed no hope of Trent ever nearing a pastoral role again. "That is one vow he should have never taken," he said.

At the risk of seeming melodramatic, the two counselors had planned to meet their clients at different entrances and opposing parking lots of the building. After Natalie and Cyndi took their seats in the conference room, Bishop Phillips entered.

Jeff met Trent in the parking lot and greeted him. "Okay," Jeff said. "It's time." And the two began their walk to the conference room. Trent hadn't had such a huge lump in his throat since he was sent to the principal's office in fourth grade. He followed Jeff into the room, and they took their seats.

Before introductory remarks could be made, Trent made cautious eye contact with Natalie and said, "Hi, Nat."

When she didn't respond to the greeting, Dr. Phillips began by speaking of the purpose of the meeting. He rehashed the hows and whys of last night's meetings, reintroduced the counselors he had selected, and told them what he hoped they could accomplish that day. Then he spent fifteen laborious minutes giving his own apology. He obviously regretted failing to pick up the signals of this misery early enough to help.

Trent couldn't help but think of colleagues in the same position. There were couples out there dying, marriages on life support, and the bishop had no idea. He loved the bishop, but almost resented the professional distance that was automatically created by church structure.

Cyndi's voice shook Trent out of his thoughts. "Trent, Natalie, as you both know, we are here to facilitate communication between the two of you. It has been a pleasure for Mr. Jones and me to be involved with you, even though this is a difficult situation. We want to help both of you through the days ahead, regardless of the results of today's meeting." After a pause, she asked, "Would either of you like to speak . . . to begin this conversation?"

There was a moment of quiet deference as Trent allowed Natalie to begin if she wanted. When she showed no interest and just sat picking at the veneer of the table with her fingernail, Trent began. "Nat. I've said it many times since I left, but I am sorry. You're right. I have acted like a jerk. I have so many regrets for how I've treated you." He stopped.

Silence.

"Natalie, this is your chance to speak if you'd like," said Cyndi.

Silence. Natalie stared at the table.

Trent chewed his lower lip and began to look into the table as well.

"Natalie," Jeff broke in, "I met Trent last night. He told me his version of things. I'd like to hear yours."

"Ask her." Natalie pointed coolly at her counselor.

Jeff spoke again. "Natalie, you two have told us similar stories—surprisingly similar. We're not here to lay blame or question anyone's account of what happened. It's just that if you are going to move on from here, even if you're moving in opposite directions, you need to make peace with where you've been. You need to offer and receive forgiveness."

"I need no forgiveness. That would be *his* need. And I'm not sure I'll ever be able to offer any to him." Then, rolling her eyes, she muttered, "That's God's responsibility. He's better at it than me."

"You know, in marital issues—and every couple has them—the blame is usually close to a fifty-fifty thing. Sometimes it stretches so far as sixty-forty," Cyndi said gently.

"That's right—it's all my fault! Everything! He gets in

161

a plane and flies away to some other place and a new job, and probably another woman. And I get left here alone. Oh, yeah. It's my fault. Are we done?" Natalie stood.

Jeff stood up and faced Natalie. "No one said this is all anyone's fault, Natalie. But *shared* fault is more realistic than one-sided blame. We aren't speaking of the past month's events alone. This crisis has been coming for years."

"Oh, and of course you know everything, don't you? I'm sure he didn't tell you about the nightmare of hearing nothing but problems from him day after day, and night after night, and date after date! Listen, I told Cyndi last night. I'm over it. I'm done. And I wish we could all just drop this charade of being nice and civil. I swear I will never spend any time alone with this man again. He isn't worth it. He's a hopeless baby!"

The two counselors turned and looked to Dr. Phillips as if they saw no reason to carry on. Dr. Phillips broke the silence. "We're clearly not going to make much more progress than that today. And I want to thank all of you for making time in your schedules for these appointments. I hope you feel they've been at least somewhat helpful. The fact is that we can't dictate any reuniting or peace treaty. In fact, after last evening's meetings, it's the opinion of our two counselors that there is no good reason to push for reconciliation between the two of you. Things seem to have gone too far for that."

And then, turning to Trent, he said: "Trent, you need to know that I receive your apologies as you have mine. No, the injuries to your congregation are not repaired with apologies alone. However, your written apology and the one you will issue in person this evening will go a long way toward healing for all concerned.

"And Trent, you need to know that I wish you well. If what I am hearing is true—that your temperament is not well suited for ministry—then all I can say is God help us! You made a huge mistake last month. No one is denying that. But such an error does not remove you from the grace of God, and neither does it remove you from the respect of this bishop. I love and admire you.

"And finally, Trent, you told me in your letter you wanted your ordination credentials to be destroyed due to your failures. I refuse, and will file them for the time being. Now, if after a time you remain certain that there are irreconcilable differences between you and this task of ministry, I will grant your request. But for now, it hurts my pride too much to think that what our church has become—what Christ's church has become—should preclude the likes of you from leadership. If so, then may God have mercy on us."

There was quiet in the room as the import of his words soaked in.

"Now, Natalie, you need to hear my apology as well. I have failed you. We lived and worked in next-door communities, and yet I wasn't even aware of the hell you were feeling at home. I am so sorry for the agonies you have had to handle on your own. I also want you to know that I will continue to pray for you to be able to open up your heart to grace. And that you will open it wide enough to offer grace to this man who has obviously hurt you so much."

"Now, to both of you: this meeting may have failed at bringing mutual mercy or any beginning of reconciliation. Again, we had few hopes that reconciliation was a real possibility here. However, Natalie, we do have high hopes that you will one day be able to hold conversations with and offer peace to Trent. It is the way of Christ. And it is in your heart somewhere, I know. It may take time, but I believe deeply in you, as well as I believe deeply in the redeeming power of forgiveness and grace."

He concluded with a prayer. Then, after thanking all parties concerned, he dismissed them, telling the two counselors that they would reconvene in fifteen minutes.

Natalie stormed to her car and drove away. Cyndi walked with her there, but Natalie gave her not a single word in return to her attempts at a thank-you or good-bye. Trent could only apologize for Natalie, telling Cyndi that she was seeing the wounded version of a wonderful person. Cyndi marveled at the variance between what she had heard about Trent and what she saw in him. But she understood full well that pain could inflict serious damage to a person—to a marriage—over the long haul.

Trent stood on the office steps and spoke for a moment with Jeff and Cyndi. He offered his appreciation for their efforts and told them he would need some serious counseling before he could be sure he had his new foundation built. "A new foundation," he said, "for a new life." He also insisted that it was Natalie's hurt speaking in that conference room and that he could not yet give up on her completely. Cyndi asked if he really still had feelings for Natalie. He answered quickly, "No. Not feelings. Just hope."

Jeff and Cyndi both offered their services if he desired, and he thanked them, but told them he would need a reference for a counselor in Southern California. "It's where I live now."

As Trent returned to the hotel, he wanted a nap. But he decided to polish up his prepared apology to Baylor's Bend Church that evening. He was to meet Bishop Phillips for dinner and then make the difficult trip back to face the congregation he had so recently and ungracefully deserted.

His cell rang—another call from Nick. "Yeah, Nick, what's up?"

"I have a message for you. It's from Kim. Her Aunt Jo has taken a turn for the worse, and she left her number for you to call if you want."

"Of course I will, Nick."

Rhonda Simpson was not typically the busybody type. But she had suspected this for a long time now, and she was finished keeping her silence.

"Bishop Phillips?"

"Yes?"

"This is Rhonda Simpson, secretary at—"

"I know you, Miss Simpson. How can I help you?"

"It's kind of difficult to tell you, but . . . Natalie Atkins just called here and asked for Brandon Tyler. I overheard him tell her he'd be right over to pick her up. It just doesn't sound good to me, what with Pastor Trent coming to talk tonight and everything else."

"Thank you, Miss Simpson," the bishop sighed, checking his watch. Natalie had left his office less than ten minutes ago.

At the end of Trent's call to Jo Anna, he heard her laughter on the other end of the line. Jenna took the phone at Kim's insistence. "Trent, Mom's glowing from ear to ear."

And Trent heard Jo Anna's weak voice croak out, "And so is this one. So is Kim!"

"Aunt Jo!" he heard Kim scolding. He could tell she was smiling too.

The service that evening at Baylor's Bend offered Trent some closure. He could only hope it had brought some measure of healing to the people of the congregation. He remembered Jeff's words from the night before, that often clergy overestimate their effect on people. His former congregants for the most part responded to him as if they understood. Many who could catch his eye would wink and nod or smile, reassuring him. Some could only look away, and he didn't wonder why.

At the end of the service, Bishop Phillips served

165

communion. It was with a strange sense of sadness, coupled with relief, that Trent accepted his position as one of the served and not as the server of the Eucharist. He felt relief that this was no longer his burden. And yet there was sadness that a chapter of his life was through; this particular part of that life had been such mystical pleasure.

When the service concluded, Trent was curious to hear Bishop Phillips announce an emergency meeting of the elder board. *Wonder what that's about*, he thought.

The elders were shocked at the news they received regarding their music minister and Natalie Atkins. There was no doubt in the mind of the hotel clerk. He knew the people he had seen checking in. The man was his music minister. The clerk had even played guitar once in his band. "I don't know why he didn't recognize me at all," he said.

The bishop thought the young man's last line was more telling than anything else he said. True, in congregations of several hundred, staff members couldn't get to know everyone; but anyone with a shepherd's heart would at least have recognized the face and voice of a twenty-five-year-old kid who had played in his band, especially one with such a severe speech impediment. Brandon's callousness worsened the tragedy in his thinking.

Brandon was waiting in the wings and was soon ushered in to face the elder board. The meeting didn't last much longer. He freely admitted to his affair with Natalie. She was so hurt, he said, and that hurt had driven her—driven them—toward the affair. And then he submitted his resignation, which the elders readily accepted. This Sunday, Baylor's Bend would face another loss.

OUT OF THE STORY

T rent had his room for another two nights, but no return flight scheduled, so he called Jeff Jones and invited him to breakfast. Trent needed to know if moving back west was a bad idea. "What if Nat changes her mind? What if she softens after a while?"

"That could happen," Jeff said with doubt packed into his tone. "But you have a job, a place, and a life to rebuild if it doesn't. Trent, I think . . . I think you and Natalie have been finished for a long time."

Trent told him about Kim and their feelings. "I don't want to run back and start over too quickly. Our divorce isn't even through yet," he said.

"You are wise to be cautious. I think you need to wait for this divorce. And then you need to consult a good counselor when you get back west. I'd love to help you out, but the distance would make it unwise. "

"What does caution even look like, Jeff? Really, when I'm with this woman, the emotions run wild. I think the feeling is reciprocal too."

"Of course the emotions are blinding. But don't let them fool you. Remember your talk of commitment. It's time to commit yourself to the process of finishing things with Natalie, before you get too involved with Kim. And remember, much of romance is fleeting."

"Explain that to me please, Jeff."

"Well, it's kind of a mutual worship thing. Nothing feels better than getting compliments from someone—I mean, having someone tell you those really good things about yourself that you like to hear. That's what we do when we date. We admire the partner to a fault. We can't be outdone at telling them how cool, beautiful, handsome—and whatever else we can think of—they are. And when someone that we find attractive and mysterious reciprocates and begins to compliment us, we feel worshipped too. We like it. Of course we do! Everything is new and exciting and intoxicating. And all of this is a wonderful thing called 'falling in love.' But *real* love is the tougher business that requires disciplined, long-term commitment—sometimes to nothing more than a promise. You do have what it takes for that, but you need to remember it. Especially when you're face to face in matching chairs in a cruise ship suite!" Jeff couldn't help but smile after his speech.

"Go?" Trent asked.

"Go. Go with patience and grace and a healthy dose of remembering what you're getting into. And don't forget this." He pulled a business card out of his pocket and handed it to Trent. "This is the number of Sylvia Cervantes. She's a great therapist on Point Loma. You won't have any trouble working with a woman, will you?"

"No," Trent answered as he wondered how quickly he could schedule a flight back to the west coast.

Later that evening, the bishop called and told Trent his car was waiting for him at the bishop's office. "She dropped it off. Said you can keep it or sell it, or do what you want with it. The papers and insurance documents are all inside." Trent scheduled his flight for mid-afternoon the next day. He would have just the morning to sell the car, but one of his former parishioners had wanted it for quite some time. And with one phone call, the deal was done. He sold it at a discount, but cleared seven thousand dollars to put in his growing California account. Early that afternoon, the deal was finished, and he was free to get on the plane.

Nick met Trent at the airport. "Great to have you back, man. Dude, you think you'll be staying with us?"

"Yeah, Nick. That's my plan. Back on the job Monday morning if that's OK?"

"Absolutely, man. Absolutely!"

As Trent stepped back out into the California sunshine, he truly felt he had come home. He saw the palm trees and the sailboats on the harbor and heard the familiar sounds of happy beachgoers—and it felt good.

As they headed toward his place, following the "To the Beaches" signs, Trent decided he could call Kim first thing in the morning. He'd tell her how things had gone with Natalie. He'd tell her what Jeff had said. But once inside and alone, he threw caution to the wind. He couldn't dial fast enough.

"Hey, Kim! I'm home."

A month and a half passed by. Trent stayed busy at work. Kim met him for weekly lunches. They enjoyed their times together, but tried to take it slowly. He was still waiting for the phone call telling him the divorce was officially final.

Nick and Allie were pushing things. The four had one double date shortly after Trent's return, and Trent could tell Nick and Allie really wanted him and Kim together. Allie wondered if Trent had cold feet.

Trent began spending Sundays seeking a place to worship. What would he do with his calling? How would he practice caring for others? On the third Sunday, he decided to pay a visit to the local hospital's volunteer office, and for the past two Sunday afternoons he had volunteered at the ER reception desk, pushing wheelchairs and consoling worried family members. Afterward he took 10 percent of his last week's pay and distributed it between a local mission and a food pantry. He sometimes thought about starting an organic house church with some of his new friends. These were all only ideas at this stage, however. He didn't feel the certainty he had in the past about starting new ministries. He was still searching.

Very early one Tuesday morning, Trent's phone rang. He strained to focus his eyes on the screen, and he was shocked when he made out the numbers—it really was Natalie's cell phone on his caller ID. Could this be the call?

"Hello?"

"Trent. I'm pregnant."

"*Natalie?*"

"Yes. And you need to know, this child can only be yours." He didn't even have time to respond. "We'll talk," she said, then disconnected the call.

Trent fell back onto his bed, both palms flat against his forehead. This could not be. And then, in an instant, he knew. *This could be.*

About six weeks before he left, there was an incident. That's all he could think to call it. It was a freak awakening in the middle of the night. Pent up something drew them together like magnets. And when morning came, neither acknowledged the act. But it was real, and now he was going to be a father.

He tried calling her right back, but only got her message. "Natalie. Please talk with me. I need to talk with you. I need to know more."

But the day slipped away without any further word. On the third day of worry, Trent tried calling Natalie's mother. She was always home, and after a full day of attempts to reach her, he could only assume Natalie had convinced her to join the freeze-out.

He spent much of the next few days wondering if he should move back east to be close to the coming child. He couldn't fathom being one of those absent and unknown dads. But how could he leave Kim? His heart was divided; he felt pulled toward two parts of the continent.

As nightfall came, he took his favorite folding beach chair out to the edge of the surf. He needed to think. He needed to straighten out his mind and spirit. He spent the first few minutes praying and thanking God for the beauty of his surroundings, and soon he was lost in reflection mixed with worry.

Entrenchment in an affair is a common obstacle to counseling. How many times had he seen couples wait too long to come in for help? When one party or both were already infatuated with someone else, it made the prospects of restoring the marriage almost impossible.

Now he understood. He didn't want his old marriage back. It sounded like miserable—if not impossible—work to put it back together. In contrast, nothing seemed more wonderful than moving on with his life side by side with Kim. It would be effortless, even joyful! Indeed, now he understood why he had met so many resistant counselees.

Falling in love is endorphin heaven—it makes life seem effortless. It feels natural and right, while working out old problems in a relationship feels unnatural and wrong. But just because something feels right doesn't make it OK. What was he thinking? No matter how much he might like to, Trent could not avoid giving himself the same counsel he had offered so many others. The ironclad right thing, he realized, would be for him to set aside his desire for Kim and plug himself back into the role of pursuing and romancing Natalie. He had seen it work.

Trent was learning an additional lesson, one he had forced upon others just a short time ago: he now knew how it felt to be left hanging, waiting for someone on the other side of the country to make a decision that would change his life forever. He knew Natalie was enjoying turning the tables on him. And he got the message loud and clear.

So where did this leave him? Natalie had left no doubt: she wasn't interested. Even following his letter saying that he would try again, that he would work against his feelings and try to be faithful to their promise to each other, she had made it clear that she wanted nothing to do with him. Was he free to consider the vows of his past hopeless? What about the child—*his* child?

He dialed Natalie once again. It would be after eleven on a Friday night. Would she be home? Would she be with Brandon? He pushed the "send" button and settled back in his chair to wait for her message.

"Hello."

"Hello. Natalie?" He was surprised that she'd answered.

"Yeah, Trent, it's me."

"Can we talk?"

"Yes. We can talk. I'm sorry I dropped such a bomb on you, Trent."

"After the way I nuked you, I consider it fair play. I'm just stunned. When are you . . . when is the baby coming?" he asked.

"I'm three months along."

"Yeah, I figured."

"Oh, you *do* remember that night?" She paused. He thought he heard a grin in her voice.

"Can you believe it?" Trent said. "Just when we had some

kind of resolve, when right or wrong, we were finished, this happens."

"Yeah."

"Yeah. Natalie, we tried for several years for . . . for this to happen, but it never did. I figured God had spared a child two parents who couldn't get along. I guess I thought God knew better than to let us get pregnant. I saw our *not* getting pregnant as an act of grace."

"Yeah, and this feels like an act of judgment," she said.

"Probably more like an act of the birds and the bees." He almost chuckled—almost. "Natalie, what are we going to do? I mean, everything has changed for us now. I know about Brandon, and I have a friend—a girl—who lives here. And I think a lot of her."

"Did you go to her? Is she why you left, Trent?"

"No, no! I had no idea she existed."

"So you ran from me? It was *me*?"

"No. I ran from being a pastor. I ran from a life that was out of control. I didn't know what to do. I thought I was losing my mind."

"What about us?" she asked.

"Us? Natalie, there was no 'us.'"

"No, you are right, Trent. Not for a long time. We have done more to hurt one another over the past few years than we did to romance each other at the beginning."

A moment passed. "This is the most we've truly communicated in five years, this conversation right now," he said.

"I know," she sighed. After another long pause she added, "Trent, I really feel strongly about Brandon. We have had such good talks and times together since . . . since you left."

"Natalie, let's be honest. You and Brandon were

involved before I left. In fact, I've wondered if this child was mine at all." He instantly wondered if he should have said it.

"Trent. I can't believe you said that. I hadn't so much as held his hand before you went running off across the country." Her fire was returning.

Trent found it hard to take this in. He had seen the coy looks and flirty smiles between them. "Natalie, I was sure you two were seeing each other. I mean, every time I watched you at church, in the band or whatever, I saw the way you looked at him. It was . . . it was the way you used to look at me." He felt a stab of pain as he recalled it.

"Trent, Cyndi said something that made sense. She told me that I was in an 'emotional affair' with Brandon. And when she defined that for me, I thought she was probably right. But Brandon and I are really close. It's almost like it's more than just an affair."

"How close have you gotten to him? Natalie, I need to know."

Natalie didn't answer. Her silence confused Trent. If he had been so wrong about the affair before he left, perhaps he had blown everything out of proportion. Could it be that she had kept herself from sleeping with Brandon? He had boarded this hopeful train of thought for only an instant when she yanked the bridge from under it.

"I've been with him, Trent. After you left, on one impossible night, I called him and he came and took me away. And I slept with him." She started to cry. "And I don't feel like I should have to say I'm sorry. I know it was wrong. But what you did, Trent! What you did to me was so awful—so awfully wrong!"

He felt sick. For what seemed forever, he could not form a word. The agonies of too many years leaned in upon him, and forced his breath from him.

Finally he was able to respond. "Natalie. You're right.

It was cruel. Over the last few days, I have found out just how hard it is to be left in the dark. But Natalie, it kills me to think that you hadn't . . . and now you have . . . been with him." The reality that this too was a result of his running was too much, and his voice broke as he said, "I've ruined so many lives."

"I need to go now," she said as she disconnected.

After she hung up, Natalie went upstairs. She had grown up sleeping in this room. She lay all alone and cried into old, familiar sheets. She wished Brandon could come and hold her. But she didn't call. And she turned off her phone so that he could not.

She was not avoiding Brandon because of a change in her loyalties. She seethed at Trent's nerve. To compare his waiting over the last *three days* to what he had put her through seemed unforgivably selfish to her. Why had she been so kind to him just now? Why didn't she give him a piece of her mind when he had said such a stupid, self-centered thing? She kicked at the covers and thought of turning her phone back on and calling Brandon.

She tried to pray, but her anger kept shoving her attention aside. After fifteen minutes of tossing, she turned on her phone and began to dial Brandon. Just as she had pressed "end," once again deciding to wait until tomorrow, the phone rang. It was Brandon.

"Hey, Natalie."

"Hey," she returned tersely.

"You sound frustrated or ticked off or something."

She sighed. "Yeah, I guess I am."

"Need to talk?"

"I was just wondering about that. I guess I probably do."

"Want me to come pick you up for a drive?"

She thought for a second or two. "No. It's late, and just

175

hearing your voice makes me feel like I can relax again."

"What got you so upset?"

"Him."

"What did he do?"

"I talked to him. He was a jerk. He said I'd made *him* feel disconnected over the past few days. That he knew what I'd been through. He said he wondered if the baby was *yours*. He just feels he can explain everything by his strange love-hate relationship with being a pastor, and by you and me. He truly thought we were having a full-on affair *before* he left!"

"Well, Natalie, you did say you two were distant. You told me that the conception happened by sheer, weird incident. And you kind of indicated that besides that, you two hadn't been intimate for years."

"That's all true."

"Well, if a guy's wife isn't intimate with him for that long, he might assume she's intimate with another. Didn't you ever wonder about him?"

"Never. I trusted him. And he proved me right! He still hasn't slept with a girl he's met out there."

"So he says."

"Brandon! You're not helping. I believe him. He wouldn't lie about that."

"Sure, whatever. Hey, Natalie, why did you even answer his call in the first place?"

"I'm tired of the tension. I don't love him! I just thought that eventually we're going to have to be able to talk—I mean, in the future."

"Yeah, I guess. I just don't want him playing with your head."

"My head is not a toy, and no one can play with it. Now I think I need to settle down and get some sleep."

"OK, Nat. We'll talk tomorrow."

"OK. And Brandon . . . would you call me Natalie, not

Nat?"

"Sure, Natalie." He wanted to ask why, but she had already hung up.

She wept and prayed until sleep won the battle.

Trent still had the rest of the evening ahead. He needed to call Kim. He needed to update her about this phone call and Natalie's news—his news: he was going to be a father.

She accepted his invitation to come and sit by the shore. She could hear the heavy tone of his voice when he called, and she wanted to be there for him. After they had sat sharing for nearly two hours, catching up on the details of their lives, he broke the news about the child. The story left her reeling, gripping the sand with her feet. This was another sudden stop in their lives together. Should he move back east? How could he be a father from the west coast with a baby in the Midwest? How would he earn a living back in Illinois, when things had worked out so well for a job here?

His questions continued to come, and Kim began to quiet, offering fewer and fewer responses.

"Kim, you seem quiet all of a sudden. Kind of like you've taken yourself out of the conversation. What's up?"

"Trent, I was just thinking the same thing. You've taken me out of the conversation. Listen to all this with my ears for a second. Where will *you* work? Should *you* move back east? *You* have taken me out of this."

"Kim, I didn't mean—"

"No, don't apologize, Trent. You have been hit over the head with a huge change. I'm just being quiet because the situation writes me out of the picture. You have things to deal with. And you have tough decisions to make. But your new picture doesn't include me. I'm nowhere in the frame. I'm-I'm history for you."

Trent didn't want to say what he felt. He was afraid to

say anything. He couldn't tell her how much he wanted to run away from his old life and make her the center of his new one. And he didn't want to tell her that his integrity might require leaving her out of the picture—like she said, nowhere in the frame. But how could he do that? How could he go on without her?

The walk back up to his bungalow was slow and quiet. They both seemed to have the weight of the world on their shoulders. Trent thought of the famous line "Want to come in for a drink?" But he didn't drink, and he sure didn't trust himself to invite her in. He was a basket case—who knew what he might do?

Kim was fighting tears. She sensed that this could be the last walk she ever took with Trent Atkins. And she had come here tonight hoping they might soon be speaking of walking an aisle and spending a life together. She wanted to be angry at him, but she couldn't. He was being true to himself. And that truth was what had won her heart in the first place.

As they clanked the beach chairs on the porch beside Trent's door, they turned to walk to Kim's car. "Kim. I need to say something. I need to say two things."

"Go ahead."

"In this new future, I have to be true to what I know is right. I have to think and pray my way into this new day—whatever it looks like. I have to. And I know that seems to leave you out of the picture. I hate that."

"I understand that, Trent."

"The second thing is more difficult to say. I wonder if it's only selfish for me to say it. If that's the case, then so be it." His brow was furrowed and he looked worried. He was shaking his head.

Kim could hear it coming. This was the "I shouldn't see you anymore" talk. She braced herself for the words. She told herself she would be able to drive home, to keep breathing, to go on from here. It was so hard for him to say, because he felt her fear. He knew how terribly hard it would be for her to hear those words.

"Go ahead, Trent. I think I know what you need to say. But go on. Say it, please, just say it." Her dark eyes implored him as tears shamelessly streaked down her cheeks. She leaned back against the car and he stood before her. A sudden breeze blew their hair to the side. "Say it."

His next words left his mouth quickly. "Kim, if I were going by the rules of my heart, the rules of the world, I would tell you something with more certainty than any words I've ever spoken. I would say I love you. Because with everything in my heart, and in my head, and in my spirit, I do. I would rather enjoy this breeze," he looked out at the Pacific and continued, "and watch the tide and live all of my days in your arms than anything else my mind can comprehend. I want you to be mine. I want us to be us. I have a heart that wants to ask you to be my wife. And my biggest fear is that some horrible set of circumstances is pulling me away from true happiness. But the thing is . . . I can't let my failures and my passion to be with you come before a life that is soon to be born. I must do what is right for that child. We have to do what is right."

Kim was quiet for a moment. Then she practically whispered, "Does she want you back?"

"I don't think so. But she did answer the telephone, and we did have a conversation. I don't want her to want me back. I just need to give this kid the best chance at a home and a good upbringing he or she can have. And the miles between will never facilitate that. But Kim, I'll tell you now, and I know it isn't fair to you—in fact, I know I deserve to be slapped across the face for this. But when she turns me away for good, and if you are still here for me, I will ask you to marry me. And I'll take you to Illinois if you'll go. And I'll even cheat you out of time to plan much of a wedding because I'll be in too big a hurry to be with you every day of my life."

Her eyes widened in disbelief at what she was hearing. But she didn't hesitate to answer, "No conditions here, Trent. You have all the time you need. I will be here. And whether it's the right way to do things in that big picture of yours, I'm telling you now: I love you, Trent Atkins. Like it or not, right or wrong—I love you."

Trent didn't know how to react to those words. He hadn't planned this conversation, and certainly not this outcome. His mind began to spin through possibilities: Perhaps when he ran, he broke his marriage vows badly enough that he could just let go of his commitment to Natalie and be Kim's. And when Nat had slept with Brandon, she'd given him what most Christians called "biblical grounds for divorce."

"Could you give me a hug, Trent?" she asked.

"Would you be willing to take one after all that?"

"Oh, yeah," she said. "Oh, yeah!"

They looked deeply into one another's eyes. They could both see the depths of affection and admiration. But neither could see the future. As he opened the door of her car for her to get in, she added, "You know, you must be pretty confident of my intentions if you think you could take this California girl back to live in some corn field." And she reached through the window and gave him a fake punch in the stomach.

She started her car and began to back away as he stood and watched, his hands in his blue jeans' back pockets. Then she pulled back to where he was standing. "What just happened here?" she asked.

"I don't know. I think we just talked all of the confusion out of our hearts, and ended with nothing logical, but something good."

"Yeah, that's kind of what I thought," she said. Then she looked at him and whispered loud enough for him to hear over the wind and surf, "I love you." And without giving him time to respond, she backed away and left him there, wondering.

As Trent prepared for bed that night, he couldn't stop replaying the entire conversation back in his mind. Yes, she had left with the words. *The* words. And yes, he had said them first. A thought kept pestering him. It wasn't that he didn't know if he meant the words—of course he meant them. But he wondered if he had let them out of his mouth and mind prematurely. He could not jeopardize his child's future. And yet Nat had made it clear, over and over again, that she no longer had room for him in her life. She had already chosen—slept with—Brandon.

A plan began to formulate in his mind. He would marry Kim. He would take her back to his old hometown, and they would find a way to make a living and they'd grow old together. He would have his child on weekends, and he would help that child grow up to do better than he had with the troubles of life. He would be civil with Brandon and Natalie.

Or maybe Natalie would want to get away from Baylor's Bend. Maybe she would want to move here. Maybe she and Brandon could find work here as well, and they could raise their child in Southern California! Maybe. . . .

He needed to sleep. He was living in a fantasyland. He was trying to worry a future into being. He forced himself to quit planning and tried to fall asleep. After a while, he drifted into a dream of teaching a small boy to swim in the same surf that now pounded outside his window—a little boy that would toddle up the beach into Kim's arms as Daddy stood in the sand and the water rushed back, pulling him toward the sea.

The next morning, Bishop Phillips called to check on Trent. After routine small talk, Trent asked him if he was aware of Natalie's condition. "Yes, I've heard, Trent. How are you doing with that information?"

"Well, I guess as well as can be expected. I thought

I knew the price I'd have to pay for leaving, and then this happens. I mean, don't get me wrong. I'm truly excited that a baby is on the way. I just have no idea of how we will handle it. I'm thinking I'll need to move back there. It's all kind of overwhelming," Trent said.

"Hold tight, friend. You need to be clear about how things are playing out over here. Natalie is finally back in the limelight, and she's playing the role of victim for all it's worth. She's telling people that you won't return her calls, and that she's afraid of being deserted with this child.

"And that isn't all, Trent. Brandon Tyler is playing the hero. Only the elder board and I know about the affair between him and Natalie. He is making this look like a selfless act on his part, stepping in and taking care of the woman you deserted when she was expecting. He's acting as if he and Natalie had never even looked at each other until your departure. I don't trust either one of them right now. They aren't making good decisions at all. Trent, I don't mean to be ugly, but how are you sure this is your baby?"

"Well, the sad thing is, Bishop, it is. I mean, we, um . . . well, it happened about a month and a half before I flew the coop." And then Trent caught on to what the bishop might be insinuating. "You don't think that the baby is Brandon's, do you?"

"I'd ask for verification if I were you, Trent."

chapter 15
Dreamers and Schemers

T rent hurried to get home before 7:30. He was hoping to reach Natalie before she turned in for the night. Her telephone rang the full number of rings and then went to voice mail. "Hey, Nat. I just wanted to talk. I have some plans in the making."

Brandon winked at Natalie in approval as she set her phone aside and let it ring. Enjoying his reaction, she said, "Why would I want to talk to him when I'm sitting here with you?"

"Natalie, how are you feeling about this baby?" Brandon asked.

"Sad," she answered.

"What do you mean?"

"I don't want a baby right now. I want to marry you and be yours and get on with life. I'd like a baby someday, but not now."

"I like the idea of getting on with life with you. But I agree. A baby isn't part of the picture, is it?" He laughed awkwardly, trying to lighten the moment.

They finished their dinner before he spoke up again.

"Natalie, can I speak with you about something important?"

"That's all we talk about, Brandon. Everything is important between us."

"Yeah, guess so." He paused before continuing, "Natalie, how soon can we get married?"

Just then her phone rang again. She rolled her eyes and said, "It's about time *he* quit interrupting us!" And she turned off her cell phone. "Now, what were *you* saying?" she asked.

Trent couldn't shake the feeling that he needed to get through to Natalie. But on his third attempt, the call went directly to voice mail. This could only mean she had turned her phone off or it had run low on power. He left a message.

"Hi, Natalie. I am planning a trip back there. We need to start talking about how we want to raise this child. Will we be there in Illinois? Would you and . . . would you want to be here? And honestly, is there any chance that we could make it? Is there any possibility of us going to counseling to see if we could make it . . . together? I know that's a lot for a message, but we need to settle some things. Please call when you get this. I'll wait up. I need to come back to town, and we need to talk."

Natalie's stomach was upset, and she told Brandon she needed to step away to the women's room. She left her purse behind. As soon as she was out of sight, Brandon rifled through it until he found her phone. He quickly powered it up and checked to see if she had a message. Seeing one message on the screen, he dialed in for it. After listening, he paused for only a second before pressing "7" to erase the message; then he powered the phone down.

Trent tried calling Natalie twice more, the second time very late in her time zone. She never turned her telephone back on.

Between the two calls, he prayed. He asked God for wisdom. He prayed for Natalie's receptivity to the message he'd left. He wondered aloud if he had carried his conversation with Kim too far. "Father," he said with a sigh, "it doesn't make much sense for me to tell Kim I love her on the very same night that I leave a message for Nattie asking her if there is still a chance for us." The self-doubt and persistent questions pestered him until he fell into a fitful sleep, waiting for Natalie's call, his phone in hand.

As Brandon drove Natalie back to her mother's home, he noticed her turning on her phone and looking to see if she had messages. Satisfied that Trent had left none, she powered her cell back down for the day.

"Things with us seem so right, don't they Nat-Natalie?"

"Yes, besides this stomach of mine that's starting to grow."

"Have you thought about, well, you know . . . an abortion?"

"Brandon! No, I would never do that! Can't believe you'd even ask!"

"Of course, Natalie! Of course you wouldn't," Brandon said. "I just wondered if it had crossed your mind in a weak moment or something."

"I can't imagine a child right now, but I sure can't imagine killing it!" she said fervently.

"Killing! Oh, no, I would never think of it that way, not this early anyway," he said. "It'll all be OK, Natalie. It will all work out fine."

The next morning, on an impulse, Trent left town and headed back out to Saint Joseph's monastery. He parked far back in the lot, toward the desert path. Quickly he found his way back to the old stone chapel. Something was calling him back here to pray. The desert sun filtered through soft clouds, and a breeze cooled Trent's face. He found a place to sit near where the old altar must have been.

He began to pray aloud. "Oh, Father, I have been running for too long. I have run from discomfort. I have run from pain. I have run from a wife, and now, as it turns out, a child. I have run from my work, where I once believed you placed me. All of it seems so wrong when I say it now.

"But you know, Father, that I ran from what was not right for me. I ran to stay alive. I ran to put miles between me and my failures, my weaknesses, and my pain. Oh, Lord, forgive me for running from the things you wanted to help me through. But thank you for giving me courage to run from a career I had no business continuing. Forgive my distaste for the church as it is, and teach me to do what I can to change it if you wish.

"Father, I don't want to run from the heart of love you put in me. It is your heart, and I love it . . . I love you. I want to care for the hurting, to love the unloved, and to encourage the hopeless. I see *you* in the downtrodden. And you are beautiful to me. Show me ways to help those who are unconvinced of your reality—your beauty—to see just how full of life you are. Father, help me to know what to do. I want to obey.

"You know, Lord, how I feel about Kim. You know that I want to make her my wife. And you know how I feel about Natalie. You know that I want to be past that part of my life. And yet, no matter what my passionate heart tells me, the deeper passion for truth and for obedience tells me I need to make a legitimate and true effort to woo Natalie back. How do I do that when my feelings are gone? I can be kind, but I can't be . . . I can't be . . . whatever it is that makes a woman feel wanted. I want to set her free. And I think that's what she wants too. So why—why must I pursue her?"

Trent was praying aloud, tears streaking his face, pleading to be released from a contract neither party wanted to keep. What could be wrong with that? He and Nattie agreed. They were done! The courts and the church counselors thought so too. It was over. So why, in the depths of his soul, did Trent feel he could not let go?

He pulled out his phone. Yes—he had a signal. He dialed Natalie's cell. It rang for what seemed like forever. No answer. Message. He didn't leave one. Placing the telephone back in his shorts pocket, he looked at the sky and said, "God, please help. I'm dying here!"

"Sounds like a desperate prayer, Trent."

Trent swung his head around, looking at the sky as if he might see God answering him in person. He knew he had never prayed this desperately. *Maybe God shows up when you pray this hard, when you hurt this deeply*, he thought. Then, shielding his eyes from the blazing sun that had just peeked out from behind a cloud, he saw the figure of an old man approaching him. And he knew who it was.

"Yes, Trent, it's me. Father Timothy."

"I was starting to think you weren't . . . you weren't real," Trent said.

"Oh, I am very real," the old priest assured him. "It looks to me, my boy, as if you have become a bit more 'real' yourself since the last time I saw you."

"I'm pretty desperate for God to give me some guidance. It's like . . . it's like I need a postcard from heaven or something, postmark and all. I really need to know what God wants."

"And the good news, young man of God, is that God is just as desperate for you to hear him speak. He wants to guide you as much as you want the guidin'."

"I've thought a lot about the 'bloody bones' since we talked last."

"Yes, my son, I'm afraid I was never much of a poet. But I can see it in your heart. You want to be true and pure. And you can't be so pure as the Father can make you unless you face your worst fears and failures. You can't build tomorrows on yesterdays that are clouding your conscience, my dear boy."

Trent felt sure that the man before him was a messenger from God, an angel perhaps, or at the very least a real person with some wonderful prophetic gift. "Father, what should I do?" Trent finally asked.

"Go back, my boy. Wherever it is, whatever or whoever it is you're runnin' from, go back and make your peace. Take white roses with you and don't waste a day. Take your roses and your pure loving heart, and offer to give it back where it belongs. Go back, my boy. And God'll be with you."

Trent bowed his head and sat silently. He thanked God for speaking through this old priest, whoever he was. He wondered for a moment how Father Timothy could have known about the roses, the white roses. And then he told God he would obey. He would leave here, buy a ticket back east, and as soon as possible, he'd call Beasley's Florist, where he'd always found the most beautiful white roses—Natalie's favorite.

"Natalie?"

"Yes, who is this?"

"It's Annie, from church. Annie Charles, do you remember?"

"Oh, sure I do, Annie. How can I help you?" Natalie grabbed the latest church directory to see if this woman's picture was there. Her name did sound familiar.

"Well, I've heard you've been having some stomach trouble, and you know I'm a nurse. Anyway, I just wondered if I could come over and chat with you and see if I could help out in any way. You've been under so much stress, with Trent running off and all."

"Um, sure. I guess you could stop by."

Later that morning, Annie Charles visited with Natalie. She expressed concern over all the stress Natalie had been under; she thought it might have been hard on her and the child. She wondered aloud if it was really a good idea for her to follow through with the pregnancy under these conditions. It couldn't be good for her health or the baby's. Had she thought about terminating the pregnancy?

Something about Annie's way of presenting the idea made it all sound so reasonable. Ending the pregnancy certainly would take a great deal of strain off her and Brandon, and of course Trent as well.

Annie continued, "And Natalie, hon, don't forget about the child! What could you ever tell a precious baby? 'I'm sorry, honey, but your father ran off before you were born. He didn't really want you.' It would be so hard for you and everyone involved, especially a child."

"Yeah, but I just can't imagine—"

"Of course not, honey. Especially because you are thinking of a real baby, which your fetus will be someday, if you don't make a decision in the next little bit of time. . . . Well, I just wanted to let you know we love you. And if you need any more information or counseling on the subject, well, that's what I do." Annie gave Natalie a sweet smile of concern. "And remember, it will be much easier on you if you don't wait until the ba—the fetus gets larger. Your recovery would be very easy right now. And Natalie, you could just let everyone assume it was a miscarriage. I could even, you know, put that out there, and no one would think a thing. This is all completely confidential."

Trent called Kim and told her he'd be making a trip east. "This is it, Kim. I have to do this. I'll keep you up-to-date."

"Trent," she said, "I know our talk last night isn't going to help you any. I really did mean what I said, and I know you meant what you said. But you've been clear with me, and I know you need to make every effort to keep your promise." She paused, and he wondered—were those tears he heard in her voice? "Do this with all of your heart. You have to go back and give this your best. You have to, Trent."

She pushed the "end" button.

He could only shake his head and wonder at what a wonderful woman Kim was. He also wondered if he had what it took to leave her here and go pursue Natalie, for whom he no longer had feelings of love.

Natalie took Annie's business card and walked back up the stairs to her room. She placed the card on her dresser and picked up her phone. She had missed a call. Trent. She knew he would never approve of what she was thinking. But she also knew it would make his new world a whole lot easier.

Knowing how difficult it could be to get a call through to Nat, Trent decided to e-mail her, while continuing to try her by phone. He typed these words:

> *Hey, Nat. I have a flight scheduled for Thursday, should arrive at 6 PM. I'll stay out of your way for the night, but I need some time with you on Friday morning. Could we meet Friday morning for breakfast, say, 9:00 at Jimmy's Diner? If you need me to get one of the counselors, the bishop, or whoever to be around while we talk, that's fine. But you have to let me know ahead of time or take care of it on your own. I'll call you when I get in. Please answer your phone when I call, or call me. Thanks.*

Natalie loved Jimmy's. Maybe it would be like old times. Probably not. He said a prayer for her and the baby as he clicked the "send" button.

Natalie was surprised she could schedule the procedure so quickly. Perhaps Miss Charles had pulled a string or two. In any case, waiting and thinking about this decision would never work. She needed to get it over with. Her heart was full of doubt—she once even caught herself daydreaming about cradling a baby in her arms. Her arms began to ache, and tears spilled down her face. Oh, well, she thought; she had two days to change her mind if she wanted to. For now, she needed to get her mind on something else. She headed for the office, dialing Brandon's cell before she left her mother's driveway.

Trent was glad to have two days solid of demolition work ahead—no meetings. He could get lost in physical labor. Midway through Wednesday, though, he injured himself when a drywall nail snagged his thigh as the wall fell away. The cut was deep, and his jeans soaked quickly with blood. As an ER doctor sewed his numb leg, he heard his ringtone, muffled by the pocket of his jeans, across the exam room. A moment later he heard the blip notifying him of a voice mail.

The doctor clipped the loose ends of the stitches—all done. A nurse handed him his cell phone while he waited for the doctor to bring a prescription for an antibiotic. He listened to the message—Nat. "Trent, I won't be able to see you Friday morning. The doctor wants me to rest. Please reschedule. Or, better yet, let's just talk by phone. I'll keep mine with me all day and I promise I'll pick up."

Trent had booked his flight online using a travel site, and his ticket was non-refundable. *She'll have to deal with a visit at home,* he thought.

"Brandon, I called, but he didn't answer. Probably at work, with a lot of noise." She thought about how dignified his old job had been, with no power tools or swearing coworkers, just professional work with people who respected him. "I left him a message. I hope he'll leave me alone. I don't think I could deal with him knowing what I'm . . . what we're doing. I don't need any more doubts put in my head!"

"This is none of his business, Nat! And like you said earlier, you're doing this as much for him as for us. You *are* choosing the best thing. Next week this time, everything will be better, and you'll be looking at a different future. We'll be free, Nat. *Free.*"

"Call me *Natalie*, Brandon."

"I'm sorry, babe—it's just that this is almost too good to be true. And hey, listen, I may have some really exciting news for you. It looks like I have a new gig. I'll tell you tonight at dinner."

She squealed a little. "What kind of job, Brandon? Oh, that sounds so good. Does it pay well—could we make it with what you'd make?"

He decided to fudge the truth just a bit. "Oh, yeah, I'll make the same, maybe even a little bit more than at the church. But just hang in there. I'll fill you in tonight."

"Sounds good, Brandon," she sighed. "I'm just anxious to get through tomorrow afternoon, and then the recovery." Brandon could hear the doubt in her voice.

"You just hang in there, you hear?"

"Yeah, I'm OK, Brandon. I'm good."

But he could tell she wouldn't be "good" until she was on the other side of this abortion. And it was vital to his plans that she get there. She had to follow through with the appointment—she just had to.

Against Nick's advice, Trent decided to go back to work that afternoon, if for no other reason than to see how the crew was doing. He stayed for about forty-five minutes. He could only supervise, and since the crew was on top of the task, he decided to head for home. Everything would look better from his easy chair back at the bungalow. Tomorrow he would make the long trip back and begin his attempt to court someone he used to love.

When Trent reached his bungalow, the sun burned bright and beautiful. The ocean breeze cooled the air, and the surf beyond the pool deck rose mightily. As inviting as the recliner had seemed on the drive over, now the poolside lounger looked more attractive. He put on an old pair of shorts and peeled off his shirt to reveal a now evenly tanned torso. He checked his e-mail—nothing. Grabbing his cell and that morning's *USA Today*, he stepped out to enjoy some sun.

He called Nick to update him on the project and catch him up on plans for his work crew. Then, after listening to the message he missed, he immediately dialed Natalie. He was a little surprised when she picked up the phone.

"Hey, Nat."

"Hi."

"So you're not feeling well? I'm sorry. Is it morning sickness, or some kind of trouble with the pregnancy?"

Natalie saw her chance. "Um, yeah. I guess it's just a little problem with the baby. The doctor said I need to rest or I could—" she swallowed "—um, lose it."

"Natalie, please be careful! Please take care of yourself. Is there anything you need? Anything I can do? I know things stink between us, but Natalie, I want you healthy, and I want . . . well, *we* want this baby healthy. Please take care. I'm praying for you." He hadn't even considered the possibility of trouble in the pregnancy.

She could hear the concern in his voice, and something odd happened: it reminded her that she was carrying a life inside of her. She also realized that someone, at least someone besides her own mother, was concerned for it. Loved it, even. Someone loved her baby. Did she?

"Trent, I just can't see you this week. I mean emotionally and all, I'm afraid it would be too hard."

He hadn't thought of that. "Nat, my ticket is non-refundable. I don't want to upset you, really, but I'd love to see you and just know that you're OK." He felt a twinge of caring for this woman, his wife. "Don't let me pressure you though, OK?"

She always liked it when he called her pet names like Nat or Nattie. She felt the tender kindness in his way. It caught in her heart as he said it now and reminded her of days long since past, days when she truly cared for him. A lump began to form in her throat as she pictured him coming to the house to see her pregnant, completely unaware that she soon would no longer be.

"Nat, you there? You OK?"

"Trent, I don't know. . . . " Emotion overtook her. "Trent, I don't know what I want. I just don't know what I want. I don't know what to say." She was crying, the pitch of her voice rising.

Trent remembered earlier days, days when they were communicating. She had once told him that when she got like this, she just wanted him to make a decision, whatever it was, and she would live with it. She often told him he was wise and good at helping people with their problems—everyone but her, that is.

"Nattie. I'm going to come and see you. If you aren't ready, I won't force any big talk about the future. I just want to see you, be near my baby and be near . . . you. I'll stop by the house on Friday morning at 9 AM, unless you tell me not to. But I *am* coming. Don't fret. I'll be one of the good guys, for *you* this time."

"OK, Trent. That will be OK. I'll see you then." What else could she say?

Brandon was livid when Natalie told him the plan. "What were you thinking? You'll be recovering, Natalie! You won't feel well yet."

"I know Brandon, but. . . . " She was trying to think quickly. "At least he'll see me truly not feeling well, and the miscarriage thing will look real to him. It will, Brandon. Besides, I can't just tell him not to use his ticket. What else could I have done?"

"A lot of things, Nat, a lot of things!" And Brandon ended the call with that.

Why does he insist on calling me that?

Trent called Kim that evening to let her know the plans. At the end of their brief, information-oriented conversation, she caught him off guard with her words. "Trent, I am talking to Jesus for you and for Natalie. I am talking to him about her health and the baby's too. I guess this means I'm praying. You have shown me the unselfish way that God loves, and I am getting better at *trying* to do that too. I want to love like he loves us. I trust you to be with her and to make the best decision Love can come up with."

Trent mused following the call: *How many Christians have such a mature understanding of faith, even after years of church going?* He pulled a sweatshirt over his cool skin, leaned back in the chair, and watched the stars come out into the clear Southern California sky.

Annie Charles called that evening. "Hello, Natalie. I just wanted

195

to call and encourage you. We'll see you at the center at 12:30 to begin your prep tomorrow. Make sure and follow the written instructions we've given you. Do you have any questions?"

"No, no questions. I'll see you tomorrow."

"OK, honey. And remember, Natalie: everyone has fears that feel like doubts. Now is the time for you to decide based on reason, not emotion. You are welcome to choose whatever you want. But I think in your heart, you know you should go ahead and follow through on this. And everything will work out just right. OK, honey?"

"Yes. I'll see you tomorrow."

The last thing Trent did before heading to bed was visit an online florist. He had two places to send flowers.

Early Thursday morning, Natalie didn't seem well. After she left, her mother stepped into her room to empty the wastebasket. She shook her head as she noticed the clutter building up on Natalie's nightstand. But when she took a closer look, panic spread through her like wildfire. The card read: "Annie Charles, Pregnancy Alternative Counselor."

As quickly as she could, she called Bishop Phillips. And he called Trent's cell phone. But Trent was still sleeping deeply in the dark of the west coast morning storm. "Trent, this is Bishop Phillips. You need to call me."

Brandon had a simple bouquet delivered to Natalie's office that morning. They arrived moments after she did, and they brightened her horrible morning. She had no difficulty pretending to feel sick. Her misgivings about the appointment nearly overwhelmed her. Only Brandon's certainty—and thinking of what a relief this would be to him and Trent—kept her moving forward. She was starting to love this baby. Maybe she wanted to be a mother. Miss Charles's words from the

196

night before were ringing in her ears: "Remember, Natalie . . . *everyone* has *fears* that feel like *doubts*. Now is the time for you to decide based on reason, not emotion."

Reason, not emotion, she chanted to herself.

Trent slept longer than planned. He gathered his things just in time to catch his ride to the airport. As the stewardess announced that all cell phones should be turned off, he noticed he had a message. *Too late,* he thought, *I'll catch it in Minneapolis before my connecting flight.* He calculated his arrival there to be just before one PM.

Natalie was shocked to see the flower delivery service approach her desk for a second time that morning. "Must be special day for you, miss," said the friendly, middle-aged delivery man.

He placed before her a beautiful vase filled with a dozen white roses and one yellow rose. After thanking him, she checked the card to be certain these flowers were really intended for her. Inside, she read, "For the two of you. A dozen of your favorite, Nattie. And one for baby." Before she could think, she swept the vase and beautiful roses off the desk, and they crashed across the floor. And before anyone could respond with anything but looks of shock, she screamed and sent the cheaper vase of wildflowers on a similar flight.

Natalie gathered herself by the time Brandon came to pick her up. As they drove to the clinic, he asked, "Have a good morning?"

"No."

He had expected a thank-you for the flowers, and her brisk answer reminded him that she had other things on her mind this morning. "I'm sorry, Nat—alie, Natalie. I've been thinking about you all morning."

"Yeah, well, I have been overwhelmed with thinking

today. I'm just trying to stick with the *reason* that brought me to this decision, and trying to turn off the *emotion* that is about to kill me!"

"Hang in there, babe. It'll be done soon."

The rest of the ride was quiet. Natalie felt steely panic as Brandon parked the car in a remote lot. She wanted to slap him as he doted over a sports car in the lot. As they walked around the corner just down the street from the clinic, Brandon's face flushed with fear and anger as he saw the tall man approaching them.

"Natalie! What are you doing here?" It was the bishop.

She tried to think of a response. Brandon looked away and studied the sign in front of the clinic.

"Natalie. Have you told Trent about this decision?" Bishop Phillips tried again.

Here Brandon broke in. "This is none of your business. Natalie has made a difficult choice. But the choice has been made. Please let us be. She doesn't need any more stress over this, Bishop!"

Natalie was dizzy from the tug-of-war. First, there were flowers from two men. Now, there were two opinions from two men. She wanted to scream, to shout at everyone to leave her alone. But she did neither. More important than what she said to these men right now was what she would do in the next few hours, and her indecision showed all over her face. She didn't know what *her* choice would be. She didn't know what *she* wanted. *Reason, not emotion* echoed again in her head. But what was reasonable?

As the two men stood steady, face to face, Natalie spotted a park bench near the clinic's entrance. She stepped around the bishop and hustled toward the seat.

The bishop's voice calling out her name reached her just as she was collapsing onto the wooden bench. Dropping her head into her hands, she began to weep. Inside, an attendant had spotted the bishop's clerical collar and was dialing 911. Natalie's mother pulled up to the curb just before the police cars.

chapter 16

FREEDOM

B randon walked Natalie inside, while her mother was forced to leave the curb and find a legal parking place. He hoped Natalie hadn't seen her. "Hold on, babe!" he coaxed her.

Bishop Phillips called Trent's cell and looked heavenward when he got his voice mail. "This is Trent. I left this message from a stopover in Minneapolis. I've arrived here ahead of schedule and caught an earlier flight. I should be in Chicago around 1:30. Leave me a message, and I'll contact you when I get in." Trent would be able to play no part in this crisis. By the time he reached home and his wife, his baby would be no more.

Trent had his plan. He would call Natalie tonight and ask if she would see him. Perhaps the flowers had helped. The very idea of competing with Brandon—a staff member he had hired at Baylor's Bend—egged him on a little, urging him to win this fight for Natalie's heart. He thought of Kim throughout the day. But he found his heart somehow drawn again toward this woman who now carried his child. As the jet lifted away from the Twin Cities, he prayed, *Lord, watch over Natalie*, oblivious to the unfolding crisis at Baylor's Bend.

No one would ever know if it was an innocent act or a deliberate protest. A young woman arrived shortly after the police left, sat down on a park bench outside the clinic, and nursed her baby.

A harried receptionist had rushed Natalie to the room where the procedure would take place. Natalie felt relieved to leave Brandon in the waiting area. He was becoming overbearing. She felt like she was in prison, a feeling made worse by the cold, sterile exam room. The blinds were drawn tight, and the metallic sinks and sinister-looking equipment made her heart race and her stomach turn. She hated medical places. The smell of alcohol and the threatening presence of hoses and masks and syringes on the counter heightened her fears.

She slid off the table where she awaited her turn with a physician and paced around the room for a moment. She pulled back the blinds to look at the darkening sky outside. A storm was threatening, with lightning already flashing in the distance, surely only moments away. She saw a nursing mother on a bench just outside her window. *Why is she sitting outside with a baby in this threatening weather? What kind of a mother, what kind of a woman is she?* Natalie asked herself.

She suddenly felt the need to muster up her resolve once again. *Reason, not emotion!*

Trent didn't usually go for the cheap fare found at airport gift shops, but he couldn't resist the tiny T-shirt in the window. When the cashier asked whether it was a boy or a girl, he told them it was neither yet. Then he corrected himself. "I guess we don't know which it is yet."

The teenage girl working in the shop smiled at him. "You the dad?"

"Yep, that's me. My first baby!" Trent answered with a silly grin.

"I'll pray for your baby." She smiled at him and handed

him the small paper sack. "I can tell you'll be a good father."

Brandon waited in the richly upholstered reception area. He didn't know if he should expect updates from the nursing staff, and he didn't receive any. He assumed the procedure would take a while, and the recovery time even longer. He settled back into his seat and tried to focus on a magazine.

With each passing moment he grew more restless, and yet more assured. Now there were no links to Natalie's past. Now they could move on. Sure, they'd have to go through the supposed grieving period, where they would playact sorrow for the miscarriage everyone would think she'd had. But that would soon pass. He wouldn't wait long to make their relationship official and make her his wife. *Now who's in charge, Trent?*

Bishop Phillips and Emma Lawrence waited in the parking lot near Brandon's car. Emma wept as she took in the full realization of Natalie's decision. The bishop tried to comfort her, but soon he found himself simply shaking his head. "It seems so unfair that Trent had no say in this."

"I was looking forward to holding my first grandchild," sobbed Mrs. Lawrence. "I was thinking my lonely days would be replaced by days of joy and a brand-new life—a brand-new baby."

"God will care for us in this new day, Emma."

They decided they could do no more to change the situation, so the bishop followed Emma Lawrence back to her empty home, then headed back to his office to wait for a call from Trent.

It was late afternoon when Natalie came walking back into the reception area. Brandon had expected her to look much weaker. "You look wonderful, Natalie."

She offered him a strained smile and said, "I'm OK,

Brandon. I'm OK. Just please, take me home."

There were no further words until they reached the Lawrence home. "Don't tell anyone yet, Brandon. I need a few days."

"Fine, Nat. That's fine. You need any prescriptions filled? Pain medicine or anything?"

"No, I have all I need." She patted her purse, which was riding on her lap. He dropped her at the house and smiled to himself as he drove away. And as she turned from him, she began smiling too.

She didn't know her mother had come to the clinic. "It's been a long day, Mom," she said as she passed her and headed up the stairs toward her room.

"Look what came while you were . . . at work," Emma said.

On the kitchen counter stood a dozen white roses, with one yellow in the center. The note read *Natalie, I'll be there soon to pray for you and our baby. I'm not giving up easily.* The envelope had been opened.

"Mom?"

"Yes?"

"Did you open this envelope?"

"Yes. Sorry." But Natalie detected by her voice she wasn't sorry. She also caught a hint that her mom might be angry about something.

But she could only stare at the bouquet of flowers, nearly identical to the one sent to her office. Trent had sent two vases of roses.

Trent caught the train toward Baylor's Bend and began to feel a little numb. He had traveled this line so many times, yet today, each time a northbound train flashed by his southbound, he remembered only one time—the morning he had run. After running so far, why was he coming back? Why was he so bold to return and face what he couldn't face then?

As he listened to the rumble of the rail, he thought: *Sometimes obedience is like getting on a train, placing yourself on the right track going in the right direction. Once they've departed, planes and trains don't turn on whims. You make your choice, get on board, and land where you chose earlier to go.* And Trent knew that for him, obedience meant riding this train in this direction on this day.

He had run from his profession and from a wife with whom he no longer had a relationship. Yet now he was traveling back toward that wife. Why? He had every reason to pursue another relationship. He felt so drawn to Kim. He loved the way she looked, the way she understood him, and the way he felt when he was with her. But returning to Natalie was the right thing. Even Kim understood that. Whether he would succeed or not, he had no idea. He wasn't even certain that he wanted to. He only knew that he must try to be true to Love. He must try to win Natalie back.

The other element of his run was his dissatisfaction with life as a pastor. And he could return this direction—he could face this day—partly because he knew he didn't have to return to that career. That much was settled: he didn't have a pastoral job to return to. When he had run from his job, he had done the right thing. In the wrong way, no doubt, but he had done what had to be done.

These things he felt clearly in his heart and soul: In order to stand before God, he needed to try to save his marriage, and he needed to find a new career. He cared too much for people, for authenticity, and for his faith to ever again place himself behind institutional walls, beyond the reach of so many needs.

He found such peace in this knowledge. *I messed up my home, and I have to try to make that right. But I was messed up by being a pastor, and I am not required to return to that role.* Miles rolled by before he remembered his message from Bishop Phillips.

Natalie carried the flowers to her room with trembling hands and set them on her nightstand. Seeing the business card from Annie Charles, she wadded it up and tossed it in an empty wastebasket. She sat back on her bed, placed her hands over her abdomen, and wondered. She breathed in the scent of roses as it wafted through the room.

"Bishop Phillips, this is Trent."
 "Hello, brother. How's your trip going?"
 "Very well, actually. I'm on the train from the city—caught an early flight."
 "Can I meet you at the station, Trent?"
 "Sure. What's up?"
 "If it's OK with you, Trent, let's talk there."

Natalie's cell phone was ringing. She let it ring through to voicemail and checked it afterward. Brandon was checking on her. "How do you feel? You are so brave!" he said.
 You have no idea, she thought. *You have absolutely no idea how brave I am!*
 As she pressed the "end" button, her phone began to ring again. It was Trent. *He said he'd call later. Let him wait.* It felt good to be in charge for once—intoxicating.

Bishop Phillips met Trent on the platform. Trent knew it was not the bishop's usual habit—he usually waited below with his car when he picked someone up at the station. His worried look and demeanor made Trent feel sick. "What is it, Bishop? You look like you're on a death call."
 "Really bad news, Trent. I'm sorry." And they kept walking toward the car. "It's Natalie, Trent. I'm afraid she has

done something . . . very difficult."

"Hey, I think we all know I'm the one who does those things, Bishop—what could she have done?" he joked. But as his friend's heaviness sunk into him, Trent asked, "Did she marry him? Did she run off and get married to him?"

"No, no. Trent, today I saw Brandon and Natalie together . . . entering the family planning clinic on South Main Street."

Trent knew what that meant. His ears rang and his legs felt weak. "What? Did she . . . "

"There can only be one reason for her to have been there, and to have stayed so long," the bishop said.

Trent squeezed the paper sack from the airport. He walked away from the bishop, needing a moment alone. He slipped a finger through the opening of the sack and felt the soft cloth inside. He thought of the words printed on the tiny shirt: "My daddy flew off, but he brought me back this cool T-shirt."

He fought tears, unsure if they were born of rage or heartbreak. He slammed the sack into a nearby trash barrel, and shouted, "No!" as he kicked the receptacle. And now he knew what he was feeling. Deep grief gripped him as he sat on the concrete and sobbed noisily.

Gathering himself enough to form words, he said, "I need to see her. She must be really hurting. Is *he* with her?" Trent asked as he stepped back toward the bishop's car, where he sat waiting on the hood.

"He was then. I have no idea where he is now."

Trent loaded his luggage in the trunk after the bishop popped it open, then hopped into the passenger seat. "Could you take me to the Lawrence place?"

Trent didn't know what could possibly relieve his spinning mind. *Help me love her, Father*, he silently prayed.

Brandon decided that he had waited long enough. He'd barely made it home before he realized he was too anxious to sit and think. He jumped in his car and drove to the 7-Eleven on his corner, picked up a box of chocolates, and headed for Natalie's.

When he arrived, he ran up the front steps and rang the bell. Emma Lawrence answered the door and barely waited for his greeting before she told him Natalie was upstairs resting and wanted to be alone.

"Just tell her I'm here, please. I'm sure she'd like to see me."

"I'm sure she wouldn't right now. She is in her room—just her and her beautiful roses."

"Oh, yeah? She liked them, huh? Well, could you give her these from me too, please?" He handed her the chocolates and walked to his car. As he drove away, he wondered why the florist had sent roses. He didn't think he'd spent enough for roses.

"Just drop me at the curb, Bishop. Thank you. We can talk tomorrow, OK?" Trent looked at Bishop Phillips with urgency in his face.

"Sure, you get on your way. I got you a room at the Sheraton for the next couple of nights. I'll drop your things there. Let me know what else you need."

Trent couldn't take the time to argue over this above-and-beyond kindness. "You shouldn't have, but thanks." And he was out of the car and up the driveway.

"Hello, Trent." Natalie's mother was cool but polite. "May I help you?"

"I'd like to speak with Natalie."

"She's resting," she said. But Trent could tell she was conflicted about the request.

"Could I come back later? Could I bring you two dinner?"

"Oh, of course not. But if you'd like to stay, I have enough made for you to join me."

"Thank you, I think I will. I haven't eaten since this morning in San Diego. Thank you very much."

As Brandon drove away from the Lawrence house, he noticed in his rearview mirror a car that looked just like the bishop's. Was it pulling into Natalie's driveway? He circled the block quickly and drove past the house again just in time to see someone stepping through the front door. No car, but someone was there—and somehow he knew it was Trent. What to do?

He drove down the street and dialed Natalie's cell. No answer. Then he dialed the Lawrence home phone. Still no answer. He parked the car up the street, out of view, and began walking back toward the home. *Does Trent have a surprise coming tonight!* he thought.

As he approached, he saw the dining room light come on behind the front room. He decided against going any closer to the house—he didn't want them to notice him snooping. He turned back to wait inside his car. He'd give them some time.

Mrs. Lawrence offered Trent a seat on the sofa, then went upstairs to tell Natalie of Trent's arrival. "She'll be down in a minute," she said when she returned. "I'll finish up dinner."

Trent felt the tension in the room. How would he begin? How could she have done what she did? How could she? This was *his* child too! He swallowed the realization that his escape and the resulting distance between them may have caused even this loss.

"Hello, Trent," Natalie greeted him as she entered the room from behind him.

He turned. "Hi, Natalie." She looked beautiful. She

looked well. From her appearance, Trent could hardly believe she had gone through what the bishop had told him.

"I'll eat with you, but let's not talk about anything important. Just catch up on the simple stuff . . . you know, our jobs and . . . just simple stuff." She was trying.

"It's a deal. But Natalie, may I have permission to apologize to your mother?"

"Sure. I'll go and wash my hands."

As she walked away, Trent rose and made eye contact with Emma over the kitchen counter. "Emma, you have no idea how sorry I am for the grief I have brought on you, on Natalie, and on everyone at the church. I was so very wrong to run like that. It was stupid and unforgivable. I was wrong for not getting Natalie and me to counseling, and I should have just submitted my resignation at the church when I realized that ministry wasn't right for me."

Emma looked at him with sincerity in her eyes. "I forgive you, Trent. I hate what has happened. There is more than you know right now, and I hate it all. But I believe down deep you are a good man. Confused, but good." Mrs. Lawrence was wiping a tear from her eye with her apron. "But I'm afraid everything is undone, Trent." And she turned away from him, sobbing.

Trent stepped behind her and placed a hand on her shoulder. "I know, darkness is all around. But I pray Christ's peace for you, for Natalie . . . for all of us."

Emma allowed silent tears to flow as she turned and—reluctantly at first—leaned into Trent's shoulder.

Natalie returned to see her mother weeping and didn't know what to do, what to say. She looked down and laid her hands on her stomach.

Dinner followed Natalie's rules. They spoke of work, but not dating. The conversation remained safe and unemotional. Trent told Natalie and Emma about his work. She talked about things at her office and how she had just gotten back into the swing of things. She joked about living at home with her mother, then reached over to take Emma's hand. Emma agreed that her return had been a mixed blessing. Trent talked about how much he enjoyed manual labor, and both of the women noted how thin and tan he'd gotten. And then they heard a knock at the door.

Emma walked to the door and Natalie peered through the curtain to confirm her fears. "Oh, no," she groaned.

They could hear the loud voice from the next room. "I'm sorry, Mrs. Lawrence, but I must come in. I insist!" Brandon rounded the corner and leaned his forearm against the entryway of the dining room. "Fancy seeing you here, Trent." Anger and sarcasm bit into his voice. "Why didn't you two answer the phones?" He fired the question at Natalie and her mother.

Trent had a way with people. Even in this room rife with tension, squelching his own inner fury, he rose to the occasion. His voice was edgy as he said, "Hi, Brandon. Listen, I'm not here to be unfair. I'm here because I owe everyone. I have many apologies to make, including one to you." He didn't even pause before he approached him and said, "Brandon, I am sorry I've let you down. I didn't show you good leadership. I only showed you how to quit—how to quit on a congregation and a wife. And . . . as it turns out, I guess . . . a baby."

"Just knock it off, Trent!" Brandon's face was scarlet. "I didn't come here for whatever show you're putting on. You're right: you have blown it. But you won't have anything to do with Natalie from now on! Nothing! And you won't have anything to do with *our* child, when *we* decide to have one. Because Trent," and now he stepped directly in front of him, raising his face up to meet Trent's eyes, "there *is* no baby! She's had a—she's had a miscarriage!"

Brandon stepped to Natalie's side and placed an arm

around her, which she quickly side-stepped as she took a seat on the couch. The room went silent, and then Natalie spoke.

"Trent," she began slowly, "today I experienced some of what you experienced that day—you know, the day you ran. And it was exhilarating."

Brandon began to smile as he watched Trent's face, somehow, already showing anger while waiting for Natalie to say the words that would mean the end of Trent's sorry involvement with everyone in the room. "Tell him! Tell him, Natalie."

Emma wrung her hands in her apron and sank into the couch next to her daughter.

Natalie began again. "Trent, when you left that day, when you got on that plane, you must have felt you were shaking your fist in the face of everything that had controlled you—your vows to me, your commitment to the church. You must have felt an unbelievable sense of exhilaration as that plane took flight and took you with it!" She looked at him as if he might say something to defend himself.

Brandon nodded at her, prodding her to the next line. *Tell him the truth, tell him what you did today, Natalie. Tell him that you—we—are free now!*

"Trent, today I went to the family planning clinic to have an abortion." She reached over and squeezed her mother's forearm, trying to flash her a reassuring look. Then she looked at Trent again. "And once I got in that little room, I felt it—I sensed that this was my chance to run." She smiled as if speaking had clarified her thinking.

Emma whimpered.

Trent stiffened, bracing for what he knew was coming.

Natalie continued, gazing at Trent. "I thought of you, with your life all confused and messed up because of the baby. I thought of Brandon and how he was consumed with anger because this was *your* baby. And then I thought of myself, feeling locked into that room ready to sacrifice *my* baby so that you two could be free to have what you want!" With the last line, her voice intensified.

Then, turning from Trent to Brandon and back and forth, she continued.

"When the doctor came in the room, she was all professional, and she said, 'Let's get back on the table, honey. We'll be through in no time.'

"I looked at her and said, 'No. No, I won't get on that table. You won't touch me. Now I'm making *my* choice!'

"She just said, 'And you are still welcome to make whatever choice you want, Natalie. It's just time you make it. What will it be?' Her voice had softened a little; I guess she wasn't the ogre I had expected."

Brandon stood confused, staring, stunned. Trent was smiling, and he sat down on the floor cross-legged across from Natalie.

She continued. "And so I said, 'I'm going to stay back here for a while, just as if I'd had this procedure. I'll stay, and none of you will tell anyone that I didn't go through with it! You won't tell Annie Charles, and you won't tell Brandon, my friend out in the lobby! Just let me play this out.' And they did. And I did. I thought I might pretend for a while, but this was too good of a chance to pass up." She snickered and said, "I think I'll finish my dinner. I'm starved—eating for two you know!"

Brandon glared at her. Trent just looked shocked.

Emma's face had brightened one hundred watts. "So I'm going to have a grandchild after all?" And she hugged her daughter from behind. "Oh, thank you darling! Thank you!"

Trent placed a hand on her shoulder and said, "Thank you, Natalie. You did well." Then he walked around to the other side of the table.

"Yeah, I know." Now she was wearing her most ornery grin, and looked as if she were fighting laughter.

"I'll call you later, Natalie," Brandon grunted as he stepped toward the door.

Trent stood between him and Natalie, owning the room with his stern demeanor. "You don't need to call *my wife!*"

Brandon made a step toward the center of the room. But Trent's physical advantage made him think better of pushing the moment further. He stalked out of the room, opened the front door, and stepped into the night, shouting as loud as he was able, "I *will* call you later, Natalie!"

And with that he slammed the door with such ferocity that an antique blue willow plate was knocked from the wall, shattering to pieces on the floor at Trent's feet. Emma's emotions had endured more than enough to leave her shattered as well. Trent was picking up the pieces of the ruined plate and speaking kindly to Emma when another unintelligible shout came from the driveway, followed by squealing tires.

Trent grabbed Natalie's keys from an end table and ran out the door before Natalie and Emma could protest his pursuit. Sprinting to her car, he started the engine and took off in Brandon's direction. "Get hold of yourself, Trent. That idiot isn't worth going to jail for!" he murmured. But his self-talk didn't slow his racing heart or Natalie's car.

Natalie and her mother sat stunned and shaken in the front room. Shards of china were shattered across the tile entryway. "Oh, Mom, this whole thing is so scary! What if something happens to one of them?" *Oh, God, don't let them find each other out there!* she prayed as she began to pace back and forth across the room, a twinge of guilt pushing at the edge of her mind. Was this all her fault?

"I'm sure they'll be fine, Natalie." Emma pulled her own emotions together in order to play the role of consoling mother. "But I don't like that Brandon fellow one little bit! He'll never be welcome in this home again!"

Natalie thought better of defending him at the moment—his behavior had been inexcusable. But she couldn't help but think about what his ridiculous demonstration tonight might mean for any possible future relationship. Why was she drawn to him? She began searching herself. *I didn't have to cheat. That wasn't like me.* Sitting down hard on the sofa again, she folded her arms across her chest and continued her brooding. *But what choice did Trent leave me? He deserted me, leaving me alone!*

And as she looked at the front door, the turmoil of the preceding moments played out once again before her imagination. A shiver shot through her as she recalled Brandon's violent exit. *Not much of a man.* Still, she feared for his safety—and Trent's.

Trent saw Brandon's sports car pull through a newly green light, cut across traffic, and head up the on-ramp of the interstate. He sped toward the ramp, trying to keep a close eye on the traffic around him, but he was losing ground. Brandon's speeding car was well out of sight by the time Trent merged onto the freeway. He accelerated beyond the speed limit, the engine racing. But he suddenly let off the gas when he saw flashing lights and heard a siren approaching him from behind.

"Oh, no. Oh, Lord, how do I explain this one?"

Pulling to the right lane, he watched with great relief as the patrol car sped past him, accelerating into a chase. Could Trent's luck be so good? Could the cop have been after Brandon? A mile and a half up the road, he saw a livid Brandon practically leaping from his car and striding toward the state police vehicle. "Gotcha!" Trent shouted as he slapped his hand down on the dash of Natalie's car.

He took the next exit and returned to Emma's home

using the city streets. He wanted to stay as far from the scene on the interstate as he could.

The culmination of Brandon's horrible evening found him shoved violently into a jail cell under charges of reckless driving, resisting arrest, and assaulting an officer. And with the fiery attitude he was displaying, those charges might increase before the night was over.

Trent didn't know what to say or how to act when he returned, but he wasn't in the mood to worry about perceptions. He knocked at the door. Emma greeted him with, "I'll leave you two alone for a while," and then hurried up the stairs.

Natalie was sitting at the end of the sofa, her knees drawn to her chest. "Hey," she offered somewhat sharply. Trent wondered if she might be angry with *him*. But before he could form the words to ask her, she spoke. "I'm sorry, Trent. I'm sorry about tonight, and for scaring you so badly with the, um . . . the thing I had scheduled today. And I'm sorry he was here." Trent was good at reading people. But for all the world, he didn't quite know what lay in her heart as she spoke those words.

"Yeah, well, I'm sorry about all that." He jerked his thumb over his shoulder and toward the driveway. It did bug him, however, that she could be so cavalier when mentioning Brandon to him. Did she not realize? *What was he doing here?* He wanted to scream. His conciliatory tone rose to a higher pitch. "And Natalie, I'm not saying I won't forgive you for the *abortion* appointment," he emphasized the word that Natalie had been unwilling to verbalize, and then added with a crescendo of mounting frustration, "but it is almost impossible for me to believe you even considered it."

"I know!" she nearly shouted at the ceiling. "I was just trying to be reasonable and pragmatic." Then she looked at him and said, "Look, I'm sorry, okay? That's all I know to say." And she quickly walked into the kitchen to refill her glass of water. Trent watched her, still trying to figure her out. The apology she just offered seemed more like armor than anything. Maybe it protected a heart that felt real remorse—or maybe it didn't. In any case, it didn't seem possible that her one apology, so hastily given, could ever produce any healthy resolve between them.

She returned to the couch. "So . . . is he OK?" she asked lightly. It bothered Trent that she asked about Brandon.

"Hope not. The cops stopped him."

"Good," she said, and Trent took brief consolation from her response. He sat at the opposite end of the sofa and searched for words.

Finally he broke the long silence. "Natalie, I'm only here another couple of days. And while I'm here, we really need to make some time to talk, and tonight won't do. I know we won't land on any final plans or commitments. But you have to admit, there are many things hanging over our futures right now. And we need to communicate."

Setting her feet on the floor, she sighed, "You're right. Things are about to change—a lot." And after another momentary pause, she offered, "Breakfast?" She took a long, nervous swallow of water and said, "We could have breakfast at Jimmy's tomorrow. We'll talk. But nothing too heavy. I'm not ready to hear about your new flame or talk too much about my life since you left." She paused. "Let's talk possible futures, but not past stuff."

Trent agreed. He got up to make the walk to his hotel and left Natalie with a quiet, "See you tomorrow." He walked in the cool silence of the night air. *I just don't know*, he thought.

chapter 17

——THE UNTHINKABLE

As they walked into Jimmy's the next morning, Trent felt he was suffering from some sort of reverse culture shock—stepping into a place he used to know, an atmosphere he used to breathe, but which now felt strange. The restaurant had originally been built by a short-lived fast food franchise, and its roof had a distinctive shape. Now a makeshift buffet table occupied the center aisle toward the windowed back end of the eatery. Scuffed plastic dishes piled high with bacon, sausage, hash browns, biscuits, gravy, and grits sat on every table. Country music blared from speakers not so neatly tucked into ceiling tiles. He'd seen nothing even remotely like this in San Diego—and he couldn't decide if that was a good thing or not. One thing for sure: cholesterol was in plentiful supply at Jimmy's.

People here didn't dress the same, play the same, or act the same as they did on the west coast. Things in Illinois were simply more everyday, while around every corner in Southern California was a postcard waiting to happen. But he wasn't here to sightsee or explore culture. He had traveled years and now thousands of miles in order to have this breakfast with this woman. And his culture-shock feeling had as much to do with the person sitting across from him as it did with the décor. After the events of last night, the two sat numbly, quietly.

"I've kind of missed old Jimmy's," Trent said as they took a seat a distance from the buffet.

"Yeah, I really like it here," came Natalie's soft reply.

After they had filled their plates with food, Natalie opened the conversation. "Trent, why are you here? Really, why did you come back here?"

"That's complicated, Nat." He took a bite of food so he could think. "To tell you the truth, the baby got my attention. That and some priest in the desert."

"What?"

"I went on a retreat—"

"I did too! Oops, sorry, go ahead."

"It's OK." He smiled. "I went to this monastery in the desert. While I was there, I met an old man named Father Timothy, and he really got inside my head, said I needed to fix my past before inventing some new future. And the more I thought about it, I knew he was right."

"How so?"

"Natalie, there are no do-overs in real life, at least not the kind where the past doesn't count. And the big deal about the past was you—my promise to you, our vows. I couldn't break them. I couldn't get out of them. Not even with no one looking or caring what I did."

"You mean that? You mean you. . . . I'm going to stay calm now," she said as she tilted her head in determination. "You mean you *could* run off and desert me, leaving me high and dry? You *could* go and get another job and a new place to live? You *could* go on retreats and cruises and get on with your life in every way—but you couldn't *get out* of the deal you made with me?" She shook her head and gasped. "I mean, it's all still hard for me to take in."

"I was desperate to get away from my work, Nat."

Moments passed before either spoke again. Trent felt he needed to let Natalie know he meant what he'd said—he didn't want to take it back or cover it up with more words. She looked at him and took in a short breath a couple of times as if she were going to begin to speak, but then thought better of it. Finally, she put down her fork and spoke.

"I guess I was always in denial about that, Trent. I mean, you were so good at your job. I've never heard anyone preach or teach as well as you. I've never seen anyone care for people like you. You were an awesome pastor! It just seemed natural for you to get paid for it." She stopped and spread some jam on her toast. Her brow furrowed the way it always did when she was trying to communicate exactly what she meant. "It wasn't the preaching or teaching or caring that you ran from, was it, Trent?"

"No," he said. "It was my inability to please everyone. It was my inability to confront people who needed to be confronted. And it was my lack of passion to spend my time pacifying church people when it's the people outside the church who really need grace and peace. My strengths of compassion and caring became weaknesses when I was promoted to CEO. My life wasn't real anymore—it became a big act.

"At my last elder board meeting, they suggested I get an MBA in church management—did I ever tell you that? 'The church would pay for it,' they said. It made me sick to think about it. I mean, I held Lenny's mother's hand while she died. He knew where my strengths were. He knew what I'm good at. And when he suggested I needed an MBA, well, I just realized my time was up."

She looked at him as if he were some tragic, impossible puzzle. "I never let you complain about all of this, did I?"

"It's probably all I ever did. I can't blame you."

"But I knew you wanted out. I just couldn't let go, Trent. I couldn't let go of the idea of you becoming this great, I

221

don't know, megachurch leader or TV preacher or something. And you could have been. But I should have understood that there isn't a bone in your body that would want that kind of attention."

"Natalie, I wasn't strong enough to insist on a change. I should have planned my way into another kind of occupation, not run off and cut all my ties. And more than anything, I should not have let you suffer. It wasn't your fault that you believed in me, I guess. I let us fail. I let us down. I quit, and it was wrong."

Trent had gone over what he wanted to say at this meeting for days now—and his thoughts had undergone several revisions as events played out. Now she had asked why he came, and he decided to tell her the truth. "Nat, I came back here because . . . if there is the slightest chance I can make it right—I mean, between us—I'm fully committed to it. I know I've messed some things up, and our situation is far from ideal, but I'm proposing to date you again."

"You what?" She slammed her coffee cup onto the table, spilling its contents onto the checkered table covering. "Sorry. Whoa, sorry, Trent. But I was not expecting you to say that. I mean, we've kind of moved way past that, haven't we?"

"Yes, and I guess I'm suggesting we move back a few steps and create our tomorrows without assuming that our original promises are empty."

The strength in Trent's tone surprised her. She wasn't used to such fervor when it came to their relationship. He often showed such passion when he cared for others, but it had been years since he'd meant something so deeply when he spoke about his relationship with her.

He was helping her dab coffee from the far edges of their tabletop, both acting as if the spill was the center of their universe.

"Trent," she said with sudden urgency. "I don't know if I want you back here." She grabbed her plate and headed for the food bar, looking for a reason to walk away from the table. She felt the flush burn into her cheeks as she stood with her back to him. Then, knowing tears were on the way, she placed her plate on an empty table and ran out the door.

Trent didn't know whether to run after her or wait her out. *Oh, Lord, help me here!* She walked around the edge of the building and stopped outside of the window next to their table. With a mixture of sign language and exaggerated mouth movements, she let him know she was taking the car and he'd have to walk back to the hotel.

He could only nod acceptance to her back as she hustled to her car. Then he shook his head. "What just happened here?"

That afternoon, Trent wrote out the proposal he'd thought of offering Natalie at breakfast that morning. He studied it, thinking that his stubborn belief that their marriage needed to be saved must seem so outlandish. They had so many reasons to give up on their relationship. Honestly, after the night before, he was ready to cash it in—he didn't know this Natalie. Questions had kept him awake nearly the entire night—what kind of future did they have? Yet something else kept circling his mind, stealing his sleep: their vows. Did they promise God, or did they not? In his mind, he kept seeing trains and hearing their loud, determined uphill chug. He thought again about committing to a direction, ending up in the place you committed to when you boarded. And he wanted to stay on this train. He wanted to see where obedience would take him.

He walked through the early evening to deliver his handwritten note. Later he called Natalie's mother and told her he'd placed an important note for Nat in their mailbox. But all the way back to the hotel, and until he finally made the phone call, he had considered going back to retrieve the note. As he got ready for bed, he smiled a little when he heard a train whistle cry out into the night.

Sunday morning, Trent decided to stay in his room. He was sure he'd bump into someone from his former congregation in just about any restaurant he might visit. So he spent a few minutes at the breakfast bar in the hotel and returned to his room. It was then that he remembered Natalie giving him a packet when she met him at Jimmy's. He had stuffed it in his jacket pocket and forgotten about it.

Mail, mainly. He began by trashing all the credit card offers. Other than those, it didn't seem that Natalie had kept any junk mail. He had a couple of notes from parishioners, mostly from the week he had left, before they knew what had happened. They were hard for him to read, and he didn't spend much time with them. But he stuffed them in his backpack, unable to consider them trash. He zipped it up and returned to the pile of mail before he could feel any more guilt.

Underneath a contribution statement from Baylor's Bend and a call for contributions from the Salvation Army, he saw a return address with a logo that startled him: the FBI! Fear flashed in his gut. Was this Lieutenant Milton from San Diego? No, the return address was a Chicago address. He tore the envelope open to find a letter addressed to him—not a form letter, not a mass mailing—and the name Milton was never mentioned. His fear thickened in his throat as he read on.

He was to contact law enforcement authorities upon receipt of the letter. He was being charged with unlawful possession of firearms without a Firearm Owner's Identification card. The letter outlined the statute: "It is unlawful to possess any firearm or ammunition without a valid FOID—Firearm

Owner's Identification card." The notice went on to mention his possession of assault rifles and describe the serious nature of his crime. Trent knew this had to be a mistake—he'd never bought a gun in his life. *Guns? How?* And then the truth sunk into him.

Three years earlier, an elderly widower from his congregation, Pete Chapman, had died of lung cancer. But Pete had no heirs. He and his deceased wife, Virginia, never had children, and they felt a special closeness to Natalie and Trent because of this bond they shared: church had become family for both couples.

Pete owned a large array of guns, a collection he took great pride in. Whenever Trent visited, the old gentleman would take him to an improvised bedroom-showroom. He would tell him lengthy stories, colorful histories of each piece. Trent had been fascinated, yet intimidated by the weapons. The assortment included three semi-automatic rifles, and Trent had always wondered why Pete needed such an extensive arsenal when he only hunted a couple times each year.

Pete had decided to give the collection to Pastor Trent before passing on. The remainder of the estate was given to the church at Baylor's Bend; half went to support missions, and the other half went toward the church's large debts.

But how did the authorities know about the guns? I left them at the house. Then it dawned on him that Natalie was no longer at the parsonage, and that he had told her he didn't care about his belongings. Everything he owned had disappeared from his imagination while he was in San Diego—he never even wondered about it. Feeling queasy, he looked through the packet of envelopes, searching for clues. Here was something: a late bill for a rental storage unit. Opening it, he found a contract with his name and the parsonage address. But he had never rented a storage unit!

But Natalie had. And she had used his name, because

she had stored his things. And the gun collection was among his possessions. Someone had found Pete's guns, and those guns were not Pete's any longer. They were Trent's little arsenal, as far as the authorities were concerned.

Trent found the number for the Baylor's Bend Police Department and dialed it quickly from his hotel phone. He was afraid to let this sit unsettled for any longer at all.

"Police Department," the desk officer's crisp voice answered.

"Um, yes. My name is Trent Atkins, and I have a letter here from the FBI."

"Yes, sir, and how may I help you?"

"Well, you see, there has been a big misunderstanding." Trent paused, and then decided to barge on into the truth. "A friend gave me some guns before he died, and my wife put them in a storage unit—"

"Your name is Atkins, sir?"

"Yes, sir," Trent answered, feeling like a child caught red-handed in some misdeed.

"And you are calling from which room there at the hotel, sir?"

"Um, why do you ask?" Trent asked, beginning to imagine the worst.

"Your room number, please?"

Panic! Were they going to come after him? "Sir, I was a pastor in this town. These guns were given to me by an elderly church member before he passed away." He was trying his best to sound light, as if he were speaking to an old friend about a simple misunderstanding. But his smile was not mirrored from the other end of the telephone line.

Flashing police car lights pounded against the sheer curtain liners of his room. Trent was about to be arrested. *Run!* his mind screamed. It was all he could think. Then one more thought entered his mind. *I'm going to be sick.*

When Natalie woke up that morning, she went first thing to the kitchen for coffee. Emma had already brewed a pot, and it was half gone. "Hey, Mom."

"Morning, darling," Emma answered, smiling as she patted Natalie's tummy. "You got some mail last night."

"Mail? Last night? What do you mean?"

Emma pressed the envelope down on the table in front of her sleepy daughter. "It's from Trent."

"Oh, great," Natalie moaned. But deep down, she was curious. What was Trent up to? Maybe he wanted to apologize for his ridiculous statement about dating her again—or maybe he really meant it. Which did she want? Either way, the letter piqued her interest.

She tore open the envelope using the handle of the sugar spoon. The note was written on hotel stationery. "Really classy, Trent," she mumbled under her breath.

"Well, it's probably all he had, honey."

Natalie tried to give her mother a dirty look for poking her nose into something that was none of her business. But before she could finish delivering the scowl, it was overcome by her mom's charming grin.

She looked down at the paper, and there, written in Trent's small, familiar handwriting, she read these words:

Natalie, this is the best I can do to propose something that makes sense for our future. It is so hard to consider, but it makes more sense to me than any other path. Natalie, will you be my lawfully wedded wife? To have and to hold from this day forward? For better or for worse, in plenty or in want, in sickness and in health, to love and to cherish, until death parts us?

Natalie, it is to those promises—our wedding

227

vows—that I appeal. I am willing to forsake all others so long as we both shall live. And now I'm begging you: will you be mine? Please consider this with our baby and the long-range future in mind. Natalie, will you renew our wedding vows?

1. *I'll move back here.*
2. *I will break all ties and communications with Kim.*
3. *You will do the same with Brandon.*
4. *We commit to dating, at least one date per week.*
5. *After each month, we have a no-holds-barred talk, with our counselors present, including:*
   a. *All of the things that are working*
   b. *All of the things that are not*
   c. *Fears*
   d. *Hopes*
   e. *What can we do to move forward, and when do we move back in together?*

Natalie, Our bishop thinks we're done. Our counselors think there's nothing left. And we have both lost self-respect because of our feelings for other people. But please, let's give our commitment—our vows—a chance! Do we believe in miracles?

Trent found himself in a cell, all alone. He was grateful for the latter detail—he didn't want anyone to see him like this. After the officers had read him his rights and placed him under arrest, they had shoved him in the back of their squad car and driven him to the station. His reputation as a local pastor, such as it had been, was of no help.

He would be allowed one call, and he decided he would call Jim Vance, his attorney friend. But the officers had not yet provided him opportunity to make the call.

While he waited, he wondered if Natalie had yet seen his note. He'd poured his heart into it. He had felt like a schoolboy doing his very best to write neatly and make no mistakes. He wanted her to hear the heart of his note; he wanted her to give their promises one more chance. In fact, while writing, he had pictured her sweet, beautiful face reading the words, and he began to truly want her back. Maybe it was just the intensity of his competition with Brandon, his desire to beat him at this game. Or maybe his prayers were being answered.

And yet he thought of Kim and her young faith. He thought of Carmen and Nick and his friends in California. As their faces scrolled through his mind's eye, he found himself hoping he could make his flight there tomorrow.

What was he doing here? In this very room, he had met with young men who were at the lowest point in their lives. In this very building, he had sat with couples seeking adoption, and wives needing their child support, and alcoholics paying the price for driving drunk. And now, he—Trent Atkins—was among those accused. He was the one claiming innocence.

Why didn't he get his FOID card? Why did he take the guns from Pete in the first place? He certainly didn't need them. And why did Natalie put them in storage? How did they get found? First the FBI in California, now here—he'd never been in so much trouble in his life. He remembered saying so many times, "Where there's smoke, there's fire." With the FBI after him twice in a month, he must look like a true felon. He'd even been crossing borders left and right this year—what would they suspect now?

Natalie went up to her bedroom to read the note a second time. She wanted to dismiss it as a fantasy. She wanted to trash it, forget she'd ever seen it. She thought briefly of asking her mother to say she hadn't delivered it. But of course that would be a lie.

It was then that she saw herself in her mirror and looked long and hard at her reflection. *When did I start wiggling away from pure truth? When did I choose something less than the innocence I've always chosen?*

She began to cry. She fell to her knees to pray, but the shame was too great—she felt naked and exposed, and she couldn't find the words. She pushed herself up into her unmade bed and covered herself with the blankets and her face with her pillow. And then, after a few moments of silence, she ached a prayer into the soft pink pillowcase. *Oh, God. What is happening? What has Trent gotten us into? No. What have I done? Me. What have I done?*

Composing herself, she sat upright, hugging her pillow. Her tears had soaked into it and now dampened her cheek. She began to wonder how she and Trent had lost their love. She remembered the brighter days they'd spent together. She began thinking of the temporary thrill of her cheap desertion of her vows; she compared that night in the hotel to the years of happy marriage. And then she recalled the fading of the happiness.

Did she want Trent back? She had loved him so. But now she felt only anger at him. She remembered all the emptiness in their home as they lived together, alone. She couldn't go back to that!

But what if—what if they could go back further and find the joy they'd once known? What if this child growing in her could unite them? Did their vows hold some miraculous magic? Or was there power in the God to whom they'd made them? She had always believed so. But this was the real world—wasn't Trent just being ridiculous? Was it really possible somehow to regain a lost love?

She'd heard of it before—and she'd also heard it could never happen. In the deepest recesses of her spirit, she felt a spark of hope. And that spark, which had been extinguished so many times, was cowering in the winds of doubt. Flickers of love had so consistently been washed dead by business, routine, and a complete lack of intimacy. Life had become nothing more than a habit, a habit that revolved around superficial success. And love had become an assumed entity—until Trent must have awakened one morning to the realization that their love had starved to death. The flame waffled again. Forever—was there such a thing as forever?

Jim told Trent there was no way for him to get back to town and to see him until that evening. Trent would have to spend the next six or more hours in jail. Somehow, his cell seemed like a fitting place.

He couldn't help but marvel at the irony. He'd done everything wrong to his marriage and his church. He'd broken the common laws of decency when he had run away; he had broken hearts and promises to God. But he had not broken any laws.

And now, here he sat in a bunkhouse cell with a few twenty-something thugs, guys who wanted to be tough, but fell short. Here he was, perched on a jail cell bed, a perceived threat to society. He had been imprisoned by the wrong authority! Or had he? He sighed—maybe he had earned himself this fate.

The others in the room were cheering at some barbaric gloveless boxing match on television. Trent hoped they wouldn't be inspired to practice on him. A familiar feeling swept over him, a concern. What was it? *Natalie.* How was she? Did she feel imprisoned? Was her room a cell, or was she seeking escape with Brandon today?

His concern began to turn into something else. How could she have done it? How had Natalie fallen into adultery—or did she jump into it? She always had such high moral standards. When they were dating, she was the one who pushed him away from a passionate embrace with a smile and arched eyebrows that said enough was enough. And when they got married, doing their taxes together always felt like a long ordeal because she didn't want to cheat the government or anyone else out of even one dollar. But she had cheated. And not a dollar. She had big-time cheated. Did that make her a cheater? His Natalie, a cheater? He shook his head to chase the thought away and failed.

In his experience as a pastor, the spouses who cheated were some of the hardest people to work with. Always rationalizing and excusing. It was never their fault. In fact, it was usually their spouse's fault, to hear them tell it. He felt a sudden surge of anger and tried to breathe in and out slowly. What in the world was he doing? Why was he going to such lengths to win back the heart of a woman who broke her marriage vows and slept with another man? The fact that the other man was a trusted friend and fellow minister didn't make things any easier. Brandon! How low could a friend be?

He'd written Natalie the note. What if she said yes? Could he follow through? Thoughts of Kim began to dance in his head again. This wasn't going to be easy.

Trent leaned back into the hard wall. *Lord Jesus Christ, son of God, have mercy on me, a sinner. Lord Jesus Christ, fix the mess I've made. Fix me. Make me real again.*

Kim wondered why Trent would not answer her calls. She'd even left a message about her Aunt Jo's passing. Was this it— was he shutting her out? She took a deep breath. Did it have to be now? Now, when she needed him most?

Natalie's cell phone rang. Brandon. She grabbed the phone with her right hand, Trent's proposal grasped tightly in her left. Her healer calling? Her finger paused over the connect button, as she subconsciously held Trent's letter to her newly bulging belly. Her face took on the intense focus of a student pondering a vital answer on a final exam. Embracing the note, she pushed the red "end" button.

Trent wondered about what it would mean to be "real again." When did he decide it was permissible for him to pursue a relationship with Kim? What had he been thinking? He reflected on the beginning of his times with her. He had used her needs, and then his needs, as excuses for them to have their talks and long walks on the beach. He had allowed his desire to speak to her about faith to break through one of the rules he and Natalie had set for each other: *no meetings alone with a member of the opposite sex.* And that first time he and Kim had met together to share a meal and to walk and talk together, they broke down a barrier; sure, maybe it was an old-fashioned one, but it was a commitment he made intentionally and with a purpose. And when that boundary came down, from that day on, everything just got easier. He had justified running from Natalie, and after that, it became easier to justify caring and sharing with someone else.

But he also had the excuse of his suspicions about Natalie and Brandon. Surely he deserved some time with a woman, he'd thought. Surely his happiness mattered too. Would God ask him to keep vows when he was so lonely and forsaken? His personal pity party had provided a perfect venue for his youthful "falling in love" with Kim—or, more accurately, his jumping into the fire from the frying pan.

To be "real again," Trent knew he needed to step back within bounds of his original promises. He couldn't let his mouth and notes to Natalie speak of "till death do us part" and let his words and insinuations to Kim hold on to hope that they might be together someday. Sure, he still cared deeply for her. But he had "caught his limit," so to speak, when he'd chosen Natalie.

Besides that, years before either woman came into his life, he had chosen to live a life of obedience to God. He had made vows before that God. And forsaking all others could never mean pursuing one woman and keeping another waiting in the wings just in case things didn't work out. No, when he left this jail, he would only remain in another of his own making until he could tell Kim a final good-bye. Not a "maybe this won't work out here at home" good-bye, but an honest good-bye. He wouldn't be running away from her; he would be running back to being real again. This runaway pastor had to run away from all that was not obedience.

And all of this would require a confession to Kim of how wrong he'd been to act as if he could ever do anything else. Kim needed to know that Jesus would never play both sides of the middle, toying with someone's affections to protect his own rights and feelings. She needed to see a clearer picture of Love.

A guard escorted Trent to a conference room, where he was finally able to speak with Jim Vance. Trent explained the story, and Jim carefully took notes.

"This will take at least until tomorrow morning, Pastor—um, Trent. I need to get some things together before we go before the judge at 9 AM. You have a sterling excuse, but a smudgy recent history." Jim looked Trent in the eyes to assure him he was not joking. "And we'll have to deal with the bail issues after it's posted—if it is. I'll have to brush up on my federal offense statutes."

"Where will I find the kind of money we'll need?" Trent asked.

"Well, you'll never believe who called me about that today."

It was a beautiful, sunny morning when Trent walked with Jim Vance from the courtroom and was greeted by Bishop Phillips's embrace. The three men began walking away from the stone building, feeling very grateful. Trent paused midway down the steps and asked his attorney, "Hey, Jim, I need to know: who in the world covered my expenses?"

Bishop Phillips laughed loudly, slapping Trent on the back. "Remember your old nemesis on the church board, Jack Sprague?"

"Not the guy who never agreed with me on anything?"

The bishop and attorney nodded and beamed. "Same one!" said the bishop. "Said the only thing you owe him is a conversation," said Jim. "And he'll buy the steak dinner."

Trent could only shake his head and follow the men toward the sidewalk. As they walked to Jim's car, they saw a homeless man leaning against a storefront's brick wall. Before the others could see what Trent was up to, he stepped over to the grizzly man, knelt down beside him, and said, "Sir, I'll be back by later today. I have a friend I want you to meet here in town. I promise. This guy can help you out!"

The man smiled. He could sense genuine care in Trent's eyes.

"Thanks, man. You're a good man. You're . . . you're good."

Trent placed a hand on the shoulder of the man's soiled flannel shirt. "I know someone who is! I'll be back."

The bishop smiled at Jim and they both shook their heads and chuckled.

Trent took in a deep breath of freedom. He had no idea what was ahead. But he had run away, and the snap at the end of reality's harsh leash had brought him home. He knew that by God's grace, he was a different man, and he wouldn't be running anymore. And that grace was enough. It always was.

ABOUT THE AUTHOR

David Hayes is a pastor in Nashville, Indiana, an artist community nestled in scenic Brown County. He has previously served as a youth pastor, missionary to Ukraine, university admissions professional, and a public speaker. *The Runaway Pastor* is his first novel and is in some measure the painful—and joyful—fruit of an unexpected bout with pastoral burnout. While much of the story is taken from true stories related to him through fellow clergy or resulting from his own ministry, David is quick to point out that the manuscript is not an autobiography. He lives happily with his wife Shelly and family, and is grateful to all of the congregations he has had the honor of pastoring.

9 780975 866214